MI

Night-Shriek

GRANADA
London Toronto Sydney New York

Published by Granada Publishing Limited in 1983

ISBN 0 583 13690 7

A Granada Paperback Original

Granada Publishing Limited
Frogmore, St Albans, Herts AL2 2NF
and
36 Golden Square, London W1R 4AH
515 Madison Avenue, New York, NY 10022, USA
117 York Street, Sydney, NSW 2000, Australia
60 International Blvd, Rexdale, Ontario, R9W 6J2, Canada
61 Beach Road, Auckland, New Zealand

Printed and bound in Great Britain by
Cox and Wyman Ltd, Reading
Set in Times

To my friend Ronald who has been a constant source of help and information in the writing of this book.

Chapter One

It had been a good evening. But then they always had a good time when they saw Steve and Sue. The four of them were old friends, now. Roger had met Steve when he'd joined JOY Advertising four years ago. They'd hit it off right away and six months later the two of them had been put together, as a Writer/Art Director team, on some of the agency's biggest accounts.

The nice thing was that their wives had become friends too. They often met for a cup of coffee, or went shopping together. Roger was glad for Hilary. She didn't have any family to speak of. Only an aunt who lived down at Brighton. And while the two of them were close, they didn't see so much of each other since Aunt Joan had taken to travelling all over the place for the Red Cross.

Roger looked at the speedometer and eased his foot off the accelerator. He would have to be careful. That last brandy Steve had poured must have put him near the danger mark. He looked across at Hilary. 'You should be wearing your seat belt, young lady.'

Hilary patted her swollen tummy.

'I can't, junior here's getting a bit too big for comfort.'

Roger grinned. 'I dread to think what size he's going to end up. There's still another three months to go.'

'He's going to be a big strong boy, like his dad,' Hilary said and lent over and kissed Roger on the cheek. Roger kissed her back and got hooted at by a grey Fiesta for his pains.

'Nearly home,' he said.

'Mm! We can snuggle up together, just the three of us,' Hilary teased, her green eyes sparkling.

Roger laughed.

But only for an instant. Because it was then he saw the red van coming across the road, straight at them.

Ian Wert had had a good evening too. A good day come to that. He'd been to watch Fulham's first home game of the season. What a load of rubbish. Still, they'd had a bit of fun on the terrace with some supporters. They wouldn't be back in a hurry!

Then four of them had gone to the Jolly Brewer and had had a few before going on to the party. Not that they'd been invited. Ian grinned at himself in the windscreen as he remembered the last time someone had tried to stop them going to a party. Christ, what a bleeding mess they'd made of the place. And it hadn't only been ciggy ends they'd left on the carpet. It was Pete who'd suggested they all drop their trousers and leave a little extra present.

Ian turned right into Warbury Road and thought about the party he'd just left. There'd been some good skirt there. Willing too. One of them more so than the other. He'd had a couple of them in the back of the van. It always worked as soon as they saw the back of the van with the mattress and the sheets and pillows. Done out like a proper bedroom it was. Something seemed to get into them. And it wasn't just him. He laughed out loud. Christ! The size of the tits on that first one. You didn't get many of those to a pound! Perhaps he'd go back and have her again. She didn't seem to mind what she did.

He turned left and left again at the lights. He turned the volume up on the radio and put his foot down on the accelerator. There was still a way to go.

And then suddenly the grey Fiesta was there. Coming straight at him wandering all over the road. Stupid bastard. What did he think he was doing? Ian put his hand on the horn and kept it there. But it was too late.

* * *

'Hilary and Roger are really happy, aren't they?' Sue said as she washed up the last of the dinner plates.

'Yes. The perfect couple. I told Roger they'd be appearing in the commercials soon.'

Sue laughed. 'Silly.' She emptied the washing-up water away and went over to the cupboard in the corner of the kitchen.

'It's nice. Especially these days when everyone else seems to be breaking up. And anyway, Hilary's never really had any family before. Only that aunt of hers down in Sussex.'

'Softy!' Steve teased.

Sue laughed. 'Well, it is.'

Sue opened the tin of Choosy she'd got down from the cupboard and spooned some out into the cat's bowl.

'Here you are, Buster. Say please.'

She held the bowl up above the cat's head and waited until the tortoiseshell cat stood on its hind legs and tipped the bowl with its head.

'Good boy,' Sue said and put the bowl on the floor.

'You're soft about that cat, too,' Steve added.

Sue looked at him and batted her eyelids. 'Then give me something else to be silly about.'

'Come upstairs and I might . . .'

And that was as far as Steve got. Because at that moment Buster let out a high wailing screech and bolted out of the kitchen, leaving his evening meal uneaten.

Roger heard Hilary scream as she too saw the red van coming towards them. And heard the urgent note of the van's horn. He realized that he'd taken his eyes off the road for a second, maybe less, and that the car had wandered badly over to the right. Roger stamped hard on the brake and tried to wrench the wheel over to the left. The red van came on. Hilary sobbed a strangled 'No' and put her hands, instinctively, over her stomach to protect the baby.

There was a high-pitched screech of tearing metal as both drivers wrenched at their gear levers. Rubber burned on the tarmac road. And then there was the more solid crunch of metal as the two vehicles hit.

Roger felt himself pitch forward and hit the windscreen. He lost consciousness, but not before he'd heard Hilary let out a cry that sent a shiver deep down into his heart.

Ian Wert had slowed the van down as much as he could, but it didn't stop the impact of the crash throwing him up at the top of the windscreen. The glass shattered and he felt blood run down over his eyes. 'Christ! I'm going to be blind,' he thought as he felt splinters of glass slash at his face.

He felt a pain in his leg and looked down, but he couldn't see anything. Everything was hidden by a red mask. He moved his hand down and touched his knee. His trousers were wet. He pressed his fingers against the cloth and felt a softness around his right knee. And then he too lost consciousness.

Hilary tried to pick herself up from the floor of the car but found that she was wedged between the seat and the dashboard. She called to Roger but he didn't answer. A tear ran down her face. And then she felt the wetness between her legs and the pain in her stomach. 'Oh God! The baby was starting.'

She tried to put her hand on her stomach to still the movement, but her arm was caught by the torn metal of the door. Hilary called Roger again, more urgently this time, but still he didn't answer. She wondered if he was alive. She wondered if the baby would live. And she began to cry.

The call to Alpha Foxtrot Two Zero was timed at 1.09 A.M. It had been a quiet night for Police Constables Jim

Scott and Bob Holloway. Nothing more than a couple of drunks and a disturbance in Hugh Street. A domestic fight that had gone a bit beyond the pot-and-pan throwing stage. 'I 'ope it's worthwhile, this one,' Bob Holloway said.

'Bloodthirsty bastard. What about the poor buggers in the cars?' Jim Scott asked, his London accent soft in contrast to the Yorkshire man's thick northern rasp.

'Serve 'em right. Probably bloody pissed any rate. I could just murder a jar of Theakstons Old Peculiar right now. Your southern ale's like horse-piss.'

Jim Scott grinned, 'I don't know why you don't go back up to bloody Yorkshire. You northern savage.'

'Southern poofta,' came back the friendly reply. 'Hey up, here we are.'

Scott looked over to the right at the two crashed cars and the ring of people in their night-clothes and overcoats.

'Christ! What a bloody mess! This is going to take the rest of the night.'

Carol Coren had been lying awake in bed when she'd heard the crash. She had been awake for an hour and a half. And, if the crash hadn't come, she would have lain awake for another two hours, at least. Carol knew that, because that's what happened every Saturday night when Bill had been to the pub.

The pattern hadn't changed for the last three years. And she knew in her heart of hearts that now it never would. Well, not for the better anyway. How could it when she knew she didn't love Bill any more? Only it wasn't just that. Carol didn't just not love Bill, she hated him. Hated the look and the smell of him. Hated everything about him. Couldn't bear him to touch her. And that's what he always wanted to do when he came back from the pub on a Saturday night.

At first she'd tried to resist, but he was too strong for

her. And then he'd get angry and start yelling about how it was his right. And rather than let the neighbours hear, or get another beating, she let him do what he wanted. Everything he wanted. Even the thing she hated most. The thing that hurt her and made her feel sick.

After it was over Carol could never sleep. Not for a long while. She just lay awake and thought about getting away and being on her own, somewhere. She was only 31 it wasn't too late to start again.

In the country, perhaps. That's where she'd been brought up. Life was so peaceful there, and simple. She remembered the stories her grandmother used to tell her of village life. Even though some of them were strange, odd, Carol somehow understood them. They were her people, people like her. Not like Bill.

But then she supposed that was why she'd married him. Because he was different. From another world. And to Carol it had seemed so bright and new and shiny.

But it hadn't lasted. And sometimes lately, when it was really bad, she had thought about killing Bill with the big carving knife from the kitchen drawer while he was asleep. Only she knew she'd muck it up, like she'd seemed to muck up everything in her life. Since she'd left the village.

And then she'd heard the crash. Bill hadn't. Too much beer. Carol had put on some clothes and gone down to see what had happened. And to help, if she could.

As it happened, she did help. She helped so much and for the strangest reason that she never went home again.

Carol was already trying to open the car door and reach Hilary when the police arrived.

'Has anyone called an ambulance, luv?' PC Holloway asked.

'I don't know. I will if you want.'

'Don't worry, we'll do it on the radio. Do you live near here?'

Carol pointed to number 27.

'Could you let us have a couple of blankets?'

'Yes, anything else? Do you think she'd like a cup of tea?'

PC Holloway looked hesitant. He was pretty sure they shouldn't give anyone anything until medical help arrived. But on the other hand if a pot was being made, there was always the chance he might end up with a cup.

'It wouldn't do any harm to fill a couple of Thermos flasks if you or the next-doors 'ave got 'em.'

Carol nodded and scurried off back to the house.

Both doors on the Fiesta were jammed closed and the two police constables decided to wait until the Accident Unit arrived with special cutting gear.

Inside the Fiesta, Hilary could feel the pain in her stomach increasing in intensity and in regularity. More liquid seemed to be seeping out of her and running down her legs, but she couldn't see whether it was blood or water.

Roger was still unconscious, but she could see his body moving and she knew he was alive. Every now and then she would call to him in a small frightened voice, but he didn't answer.

Outside, Hilary could see the shapes of people watching and hear the sound of the rescue activity. A policeman's head appeared at the window and shouted, 'Are you all right?'

She shook her head and pointed at her stomach.

'My baby! My baby!' she shouted back.

'We're doing what we can,' he said and moved away again.

Hilary told herself to stay calm. Like Sister Anne had taught her at convent school. Sister Anne and St Mary Divines were what she always thought about in any kind of crisis. But then that was hardly surprising since for so many years the two of them had played such a large part in her life.

There were many times when Aunt Joan couldn't have her for the holidays. And then she had had to stay in the convent with Sister Anne all summer long. And once or twice over Christmas as well.

Sister Anne had been kind but very quiet. And that in turn had meant that Hilary had become very quiet too. It had taken Roger to bring her out of herself again.

Roger with his good commonsense. And his kindness. And his patience. She wished Roger could talk to her now.

She wished they would hurry up and get her out of the car. Every minute she stayed there cramped up, her stomach pressing against the hardness of wood and metal, endangered the baby's life. She knew she ought to stay calm but something inside her head made her want to scream so they'd come and get her out.

Bob Holloway and Jim Scott had got the door of the red van open, the tortured metal finally giving way under the combined weight of the two bulky police constables. 'Blimey, he doesn't look too good, does he?' Jim Scott asked.

'Right mess. Another bloody uniform. I've only just got it back after that sodding drunk threw up all over me. Come on, let's see if we can move the poor bastard,' Bob Holloway replied and started to pull Ian Wert out of the van.

As the body started to come free, Jim Scott put his arms under Wert's thighs and together the two policemen put the still, unconscious body down on one of Carol Coren's blankets.

Carol put another blanket over the body and mopped away a bit of the blood from the young man's face.

'Are you all right here for a minute, luv?' PC Holloway asked. Carol nodded.

'Good lass.'

By now another police car, the police accident unit and an ambulance from St Michael's Hospital had arrived. The crowd had grown too. Lights were on up and down the street and other cars had stopped.

Holloway and Scott busied themselves asking if anyone had seen the accident. Or if anyone knew either of the drivers. But no-one had seen anything.

By the time the accident unit had cut through the twisted metal of the Fiesta door, Hilary was at her wits' end.

The baby was moving and the wetness between her legs was getting worse. Her breathing was irregular and the pains in her stomach hurt her. The ambulance men started to move her and Hilary cried out again. This time it was from the pain in her shoulder. She began to cry again. She wished her Roger were beside her.

The ambulance men lifted Hilary on to a stretcher and carried her to the ambulance. A woman was walking beside the stretcher talking to her, telling her to calm down, assuring her it would be all right. It was Carol Coren.

Inside the ambulance a doctor made a quick examination of her and asked a few questions. Hilary answered between sobs.

'I'm going to give you an injection,' the doctor said. 'It won't hurt, it's just to help you relax until we get you to the hospital.'

Hilary felt her dress being pulled up over her stomach and the prick of the syringe as it entered her thigh. 'Where's Roger, what's happened to Roger?' she asked as almost immediately she felt herself drifting off to sleep.

Roger was on a stretcher, still unconscious, but otherwise not badly hurt. He had minor cuts on his face and hands. And Dr Willis was ready to diagnose a case of concussion, but in a crash like this one, it was a small price to pay.

Ian Wert wasn't so lucky. His face was not going to be a

pretty sight, poor devil. But his eyes were all right. And the knee that looked such a mess was mainly cuts from the broken glass of the windscreen.

A second ambulance arrived and soon all three survivors were on their way to St Michael's Hospital.

At the scene of the accident PCs Scott and Holloway started measuring skid marks and drawing up a diagram of the position of both vehicles. The accident unit had already taken photographs. And very soon a local garage pick-up truck was on its way to bring in two more.

People drifted back to their homes. Lights went out and Carol Coren gave PC Bob Holloway a cup of tea from the vacuum flask and cadged a lift to the hospital, making the excuse that she wanted to get back her blankets.

What she really wanted was somewhere to spend the rest of the night before starting a new life the next morning. She was also curious to know how the woman made out. Something in Hilary had cried out to Carol. Something Carol couldn't explain. Maybe it was the pain that Carol understood so well. But maybe it was something more.

And there was something else too. Carol didn't understand it, but the woman was strangely familiar. But try as she might, Carol couldn't think why, or where, if they'd met before, it could have been. Maybe it would come to her later. And that was another reason why she had to go to the hospital.

Chapter Two

St Michael's Hospital had been built in 1923. It was an ugly building when it was opened, by the then Lord Ellesmere, and the many sprawling additions that had made their appearance over the next 60 years had done nothing to improve the look of the place. But as many agreed, it did! And from the state of the economy it would have to go on doing for a few more years yet.

After all it had seen its way through a world war and a host of minor epidemics and local emergencies.

The inside of the hospital was as dark and as gloomy as the outside. Even the standard issue white paint and the new fluorescent lights had failed to make much difference to the place. But the walls were thick and solid and if the equipment wasn't exactly new, it worked efficiently enough.

The hospital still managed to deal with over twenty thousand bed patients a year. And the casualty department dealt with a never ending succession of burns, broken bones, fingers stuck in bottles, blisters, boils and the beatings that men and women handed to their lovers, friends, wives, husbands, and sundry relations.

Hilary was logged in at 1.42 A.M. and taken straight to the operating theatre. During the journey she had become restless, despite the injection given her by Dr Willis. She had started talking and then shouting. It was as if she was having a furious conversation with someone they couldn't see. But it was the tongue she spoke in that was the strangest part of all.

Dr Willis was an educated man, with a working knowledge of several languages, and one of the nurses, an Iranian girl, spoke several middle-eastern tongues, but neither recognized the words that Hilary poured out.

The atmosphere in the back of the ambulance had been strange. They had all felt it. Even Jack Drop, the driver, partitioned off in the front, had felt it. He'd driven faster than usual, but not as well. He said afterwards that he'd felt as if someone was looking over his shoulder urging him to go faster. It had made him nervous. And twice he'd nearly misjudged a corner.

The young Iranian nurse had been affected most of all. She'd felt that Hilary was in danger and that, in some mysterious way, all of them were being threatened too. She'd said a silent prayer to Allah and added one to the Ayatollah Khomeini just to be on the safe side.

The journey hadn't taken long. But all of them were pleased when they'd arrived back at gloomy old St Michael's.

Hilary had been taken out first, and then Jack and Ken Wilsner returned for Ian Wert. Dr Willis had radioed ahead for the operating theatre to be made ready. He had become more and more concerned about Hilary's condition and increasingly believed that some kind of help would be needed in the premature birth of Hilary's unborn child.

Examination of Ian Wert showed that his face was severely cut but that his eyesight was unaffected. It was Dr Willis's view that even with extensive plastic surgery Ian Wert's face would never again be a very attractive sight.

As for the knee, well, that would heal. Some glass had been removed. But no doubt there was more, which could only be dealt with under better conditions. The leg wasn't a problem. There would be a scar. An ugly one, but the knee would mend and the leg would function normally.

Roger was in a second ambulance still unconscious and blissfully unaware of the dramas surrounding him and the crash. The doctor had looked at him, briefly, and was satisfied that there was no apparent severe injury. It was only a question of time before he regained consciousness.

The police were anxious to question all three occupants of the two vehicles. From the position of the car and the van it was almost impossible to tell what had happened. There had been no overwhelming smell of alcohol in either the car or the van but this didn't mean that neither driver had been drinking. But there was nothing the police could do. Only wait. And in the view of the doctor that might be a long job. As Bob Holloway said: 'It's a right bloody caper we've fallen into 'ere, mate.' And he settled down on one of the hard chairs in the casualty department that commanded a good view of the rather pretty blonde nurse on duty there.

Hilary was only dimly aware of what was happening to her. She remembered the crash and the cries and people finally getting her out of the car. And now she was aware that people were taking her clothes off. She was also aware of voices, hushed, but anxious. And she knew they were concerned about her. And the baby.

It was the baby the other voice was worried about. The other voice that spoke in a tongue Hilary didn't understand: but yet she did. And all the time it said the same thing. The baby! The baby! Don't let them take my baby!

Hilary was aware of herself answering the voice. Arguing that they weren't going to hurt the baby. And that anyway it was Hilary's baby. The baby she and Roger had made together. It was their baby. But the voice didn't stop. It became more and more insistent that Hilary fight. Fight for the baby's life. The baby that belonged to 'It'. Whoever it was. In vain Hilary begged and pleaded, shouted, but the voice, It, gave her no peace.

The pain had gone now. She supposed it was the injection. But she could still feel little Roger moving about. And there was still the wetness. She felt her legs being parted as a nurse started to shave her. And she realized that they must be going to deliver the baby prematurely.

The voice urged her to stop them. Hilary didn't know what to do. She wasn't a strong person. She wished Roger was there. She tried to call his name but it sounded funny. Not like Roger, but like something foreign. And Hilary knew that it was the voice that was stopping her.

Carol didn't quite know why she'd told the lie, except there was this feeling. Well, two feelings really. The first was that somehow she knew Hilary and the second was that Hilary was in some kind of trouble.

Carol had 'had feelings' all her life. Just as her mother had. But then that was part of the village. That was all part of the stories they told.

Village stories! Was that how she knew Hilary? Surely not. It would be too much of a coincidence. But there was this feeling.

And they were never wrong. When she'd told Bill and other people about her feelings they'd laughed at her. So after a while she'd kept them to herself.

There were lots of times when she could have told them something bad was going to happen, but if they wouldn't listen, that was their look-out.

There was the time she'd tried to tell Bill's sister May about the baby, but she hadn't listened. And two days later the baby had been stung to death in its pram by a swarm of bees.

Carol didn't know what she was going to do about Hilary Wright at the moment. She just knew that she had to be near her.

By the time they'd finished taking the glass out, Ian Wert's face looked like a piece of minced steak. Large flaps of skin hung loosely over one cheek and by his left eye. There were splits in the skin in half a dozen other places. It took 123 stitches to close the wounds. And when it was finished, the young man's face looked like a railway map.

They bandaged him up leaving just a narrow slit for the eyes and the mouth, and put him under heavy sedation. It would be another twenty-four hours, at least, before PCs Holloway and Scott could start to question him about the accident.

Roger's minor cuts and abrasions had been attended to. It was the work of minutes rather than the hours needed on Ian Wert's face. On the outside there was nothing to worry about. Roger Wright was, or would be, as good as new.

It was what was happening on the inside that was worrying the doctors at the moment. Roger was still unconscious and appeared to be suffering from severe concussion. But until he regained consciousness the extent of any internal brain damage could not be diagnosed. The police could not question him, and more importantly, nor could Dr Willis consult him about Hilary and the baby.

Attempts to trace any of Hilary's relatives had failed. But this was hardly surprising since the girl's family consisted of one Aunt Joan, who was away in Africa on some kind of missionary visit. It was Aunt Joan who had taken Hilary in at the age of 10 when her parents had died, and acted as mother, father and friend to her, when she could, for the next ten years.

Roger's parents had been identified and were on their way to the hospital, but they didn't help Dr Willis. A more detailed examination of the patient had shown that the accident had affected the foetus, and its position in the womb, more seriously than he'd thought at first. And then there was the condition of the mother. She was in shock and displaying signs of emotional disturbance to a degree that he had not experienced in 25 years of medicine.

Having said that, problems were rare these days, even

in the case of a premature birth like this. An incubator was standing by and every precaution that modern science could supply had been taken. Even so, Dr Willis was uneasy. The scene in the ambulance, the conversation in a strange tongue with a person or persons unseen, had disturbed him more than he'd cared to admit in front of the little Iranian nurse and the others.

In view of her excited state, Dr Willis had decided to put Hilary Wright under a general anaesthetic. That way at least he stood a chance of delivering the baby without hindrance from the patient.

He looked at his watch. He could not delay much longer. If there was a choice to make between mother and baby then he would have to follow the guidelines laid down by the BMA. And that meant mother came first. Not that, in his experience, any relative or spouse had ever made any other decision.

In the waiting room Carol Coren felt herself grow tense. And she knew that whatever was troubling Hilary Wright was reaching its height. She could feel electricity in the air. An expectancy, at once exciting and ominous.

Further down the corridor Mr and Mrs Wright, senior, sat silently waiting for the smallest piece of news. A nurse had brought Judith Wright a cup of tea. Judith lifted it, with both hands so as not to spill the lukewarm liquid.

'Do you think they'll be all right, Lionel?' she asked, her voice shaking almost as much as her hands.

'Course they will, love,' he said without any great conviction.

'It would have been our first grandchild.'

'It still will, my dear. You'll see.'

Judith Wright didn't say anything. She just nodded. She'd known something was wrong before she went to bed. But Lionel had told her not to be silly. And then the phone had rung, and she'd known it was trouble. She remembered from the war, no good news ever came when the phone rang at night.

That was when they'd heard her brother Peter had been killed in action. He was only 20. A Second Lieutenant in the Dragoon Guards. Apart from Lionel and Roger, he was the only person Judith had ever cared about. Her parents had been remote figures who had seemed vaguely embarrassed at having produced two children. Since she'd been married herself Judith had often wondered whether those were the only two occasions on which her parents had made love.

Lionel shifted his weight on the chair. His back was bad these days and it was difficult for him to sit in one position for long. He hoped to God Roger was going to be all right. And Hilary too, for that matter. It wasn't just because Roger was his son. He knew that if anything happened to the boy, Judith would never be the same again. He remembered when her brother Peter had been killed in the war, she'd grieved for months. And when Judith grieved, life was distinctly uncomfortable for everyone around.

Hilary only half heard what the doctor said to her. She understood they were going to deliver the baby prematurely and that they needed to give her a general anaesthetic. But then *the* voice had got louder and more urgent. The Baby! The Baby! Don't let them take the Baby! And she had tried to explain, but the voice wouldn't listen. Nor would it answer when she asked who it was, or what it was. And the struggle in her head and in her body got worse. They gave her another injection to quieten her, put her on a trolley and wheeled her down to the operating theatre.

Albert Stowell was 48. He had been an anaesthetist for 23 years. And for the last 10 years he had been at St

Michael's for every major operation the hospital had carried out. Albert was very precise. As was Marjorie his wife. And their preciseness was apparent in their luxury bungalow. For a start its very position was precise. It stood square on its ground, the front facing due north, the back due south. The garden surrounding the bungalow was laid out with almost military precision. There were, for example, exactly the same number of pansies on either side of the front path. And each pansy was exactly the same distance from the next. And each lined up directly opposite its counterpart on the other side of the path.

And it didn't stop there, this obsession with the symmetrical, the geometric. The inside of their bungalow followed the same mathematical rules. Each piece of furniture sitting square in its fixed position, never moving, never changing.

In fact, the only imprecise part of Albert Stowell's life was his job. Or to be precise his working hours. They were never the same from one day to the next. And strangely he didn't mind.

Take this particular case for example. He and Marjorie had been asleep in their twin beds when the phone had rung, and now, here he was with this poor young girl (she couldn't have been more than 23) putting her under so that she could have her baby. And what a fuss she was making about it.

All that talking in a strange tongue. It made you feel funny. The nurses could feel it, too. You could see that. What a carry-on to tell Marjorie about. Still, she was pretty, this young girl. She had a very symmetrical face. He'd noticed that right away.

But then he mustn't think about that. They were ready. He watched Dr Willis, what an untidy man he was, start on the delicate job in hand.

In the rest of the hospital everything was quiet. Well,

nearly quiet. PC Holloway occasionally said something to PC Scott. Mrs Wright cried and night nurses spoke in hushed tones only when they needed to. There was no change in the condition of patients Wright or Wert.

In the maternity ward, Mrs O'Reilly was still awake, but she was not making any noise. She was thinking of her other six children and their drunken sod of a father and wondering how she had come to be in here again, only a year after the last visit.

If only the Father would say it was all right to use contraceptives, instead of 'leaving it to your conscience, my child. I'm sure you'll come to the right decision'. A fine bloody help, that was. 'Oh sorry, Father,' she said to herself.

Well this was going to be the last. Seven kids was enough for anyone. She'd done her bit to see that the true religion was passed on. It was up to someone else now. If it happened again she was going to get rid of it, even if she had to do it herself. She'd heard of a woman who'd managed very well with a sharp knitting needle. It was only blood and a bit of something else, after all.

In the operating theatre things had changed. Dr Willis was fighting to save the life of the baby without putting the mother at risk. But he knew, sooner or later, he was going to have to make the decision he hated making. Mother or child. An age old debate that thank God was becoming a rarity. It would have to fall to him. He knew other doctors to whom the decision would mean nothing. It was a clinical decision. They were not God, merely God's instrument. That was the theory. And it was right.

But it was not that easy for Dr Willis. And hadn't been since he'd lost his wife in childbirth. And then the child, never very strong, had died at an early age. Not that anyone could have done anything. It had all been a good deal less easy 30 years ago.

Not that this one was easy. Why was the damn girl fighting him like this? And then the decision was taken out of Dr Willis's hands. There was nothing more he could do. Suddenly the thing was there.

And thing was the only word to describe it. Because it was like no other baby, premature or otherwise, that Dr Willis had ever seen. Albert Stowell gasped. The two theatre nurses stepped back in horror. And even Dr Willis had to look away. Hilary moaned. A low, unpleasant sound that came from deep in her throat.

The thing on the operating table jerked convulsively. Its odd shaped limbs and curious twisted body seeming to move all at once. And in different directions.

And then it let out a terrible sound. Not just a scream, but a thin, wailing, screeching sound full of agony and, somehow, full of menace too.

It was a sound that seemed to find its way to every corner of the old, dark hospital. And even while the cry was still echoing round the white and green corridors, the thing, half-animal, half-human, died.

If the cry was heard everywhere in the hospital, and it was, then the death was felt too. In the maternity ward Mrs O'Reilly crossed herself and swore to God that she hadn't meant what she'd said earlier about getting rid of the next baby herself.

Other mothers in the ward woke and worried about their babies born and unborn. And the babies themselves started to cry. Thin wailing sounds that echoed the terrible scream from the operating theatre.

In other wards, patients suddenly awake reached above their beds and rang the bells and buzzers that summoned the nurse. It was not possible to be certain, but as far as anyone could judge, two more patients died at the same time as the thing passed away. It was as if he, or it, was unwilling to make its long, dark journey to the other side alone.

The scream even penetrated Roger's unconscious brain. He turned uneasily in his coma. A fierce sweat broke out all over him. And his lips formed words that no-one could hear. A nurse stood uneasily by his side, but soon the restlessness passed and he sank back into a deep sleep.

The effect of the scream on Ian Wert was more violent. He rose up in his bed like some half-crazed, half-bandaged mummy and started to tear at the bandages as if they were strips of red-hot metal burning into his torn flesh. Nurse Hislop tried to stop him but he was too strong for her. She opened the door and cried out for help to the two constables. It took both of them to hold Wert down while Dr Barlow gave him a second injection.

'There's something bloody strange going on in this hospital if you ask me,' Bob Holloway observed when they were outside again.

'Brilliant. Give the man a prize. He's a genius.'

'Well, it's giving me the creeps and I don't mind admitting it. I'd rather deal with a good, honest villain any day.'

'What do you think it was screamed?' Jim Scott asked his partner.

'Nothing human. Not that noise.'

'Do you think we ought to see if anything's the matter?' Jim Scott asked.

'Aye. Let's see if we can find out who's in charge. It'll be better than doing nowt.'

The two other people most affected by the scream and the subsequent death of the thing each reacted in entirely different ways. Judith Wright had seen danger and unhappiness for her son, the other, Carol Coren, had sensed that in the tragedy was something that would help her find a role in life. And that somehow, maybe quite soon, she would be needed to help. But until then she needed somewhere to live and something to live on.

She looked at her watch. It was nearly 3 o'clock in the morning. Bill would still be asleep. She wondered if she dared risk it. There was money in the house. Not a lot, but enough to keep her going, if she was careful, for two or three weeks. It was the money she'd put by for some new clothes. She'd hidden it in the wardrobe in an old pair of shoes she hardly ever wore. She knew that if Bill found it he wouldn't be sober for days. And she didn't dare think about what he might force her to do then.

She put her coat on and slipped out of the hospital. There was a cab passing and she got it to drop her at the end of her road. At the front gate she took off her shoes, just in case Bill heard her on the front path. Slowly she put the key in the lock and pushed the door open. Everything was as she had left it. Everything was quiet. She tip-toed up the stairs, missing out the fifth one altogether. It was the one that creaked. The one that always told her Bill was near.

At the bedroom she dropped on to all fours so that Bill wouldn't see her from the bed, and slowly, very slowly, inched her way towards the wardrobe.

On the bed Bill Coren stirred in his sleep and flung an arm over the adjoining pillow. Carol froze in her tracks. But there was no further movement and two minutes later she was at the wardrobe. The door swung open, silently. Carol reached to the back of the cupboard and carefully, oh so carefully, picked up the left, black, court shoe and drew it towards her.

The money was there, where she'd left it. She pulled the notes out of the shoe, slipped them into her coat pocket, and started to inch her way back towards the bedroom door. But it was harder going backwards and Carol's left foot caught the leg of the dressing-table stool and sent it clattering back against the table.

The light went on and in less than thirty seconds Carol found herself looking up at the naked form of her husband.

'What are you doing, Carol love?' Bill Coren asked with

an evil grin on his face. 'You're not thinking of going somewhere, surely?'

Carol started to back away, but found herself stopped by the wall.

'Well answer, luv,' her husband said stroking her hair as he stood over her. 'You're not frightened of Bill, are you?'

Carol tried to answer, but all that came out was a thin whispering sound.

'Look up at me,' Bill commanded.

Slowly, Carol lifted her head. He was standing right above her now and she found herself looking at his rapidly swelling phallus.

'Carol's going to be nice to Bill now. Otherwise Bill's going to get cross. And Carol wouldn't like that, would she?'

'No Bill, please Bill,' Carol begged.

Bill laughed. It was a coarse ugly sound.

'You know what to do, Carol.'

'No Bill, not that. Please . . .' the word trailed off in a long sigh of despair. She had been so certain it would be all right this time. She had been so near.

'Carol, I'm waiting, luv. But I'm not going to wait much longer without losing my temper.'

Slowly she forced herself to rise to her knees and take his huge member into her mouth.

'That's a good girl, Carol,' her husband said.

It was the last time that Bill Coren ever spoke those words. Because it was then that Carol struck. Savagely she bit with all her strength. And she kept on biting, harder and harder as she felt the blood flow into her mouth and run down her chin.

In vain her husband tried to tear her away, but she was like a cat that had a rat by the throat. Her mouth opened and closed again, this time biting deeply into his left testicle. Bill Coren screamed with pain. And the scream somehow told Carol that now was the time to go. This time for good. She pushed her husband to one side, picked up her coat and ran as fast as she could down the stairs and out of the house.

Chapter Three

It was 11 o'clock in the morning and Judith Wright was still in bed. She had sipped at a cup of tea her husband had brought her, but she had left the thin slices of toast he'd cut specially. She had been in bed for two days. Ever since the accident. And even the news that Roger had recovered consciousness had done nothing to lift the acute melancholia that had afflicted her from the time she'd heard the scream.

The doctor in the hospital had given her something to quieten her down and advised Lionel to take her home. Just before they left, Lionel had been told that the child had died during birth. Lionel had told Judith later. But she'd said she already knew. Lionel supposed they'd all known really. The scream could only have been the sound of someone, or something, dying.

Something. Why had he said something? Lionel shook his head. He was getting fanciful now, like Judith.

On the way home from the hospital she had gone on about a voice and Roger being in danger. Lionel had put it down to hysteria and the fact that Judith had always been an emotional person.

That's where they were so different. Perhaps that's why things hadn't been too good recently. When they'd first met, Judith's beauty, her life, her sense of fun had been so great that Lionel had overcome his natural reserve and shyness, because he knew that Judith was the only person in the world for him.

And much to his surprise, he had found that she felt the same way about him. She had liked his quietness and his strength. The two of them had complemented each other.

And, of course, Lionel thought, there had been the physical side of things, too. That had been good between them, from the beginning.

But that hadn't lasted into middle age. Perhaps it never did, although Lionel was sure that somewhere deep inside her Judith still had the need and the desire. He knew he did. But somehow the two of them couldn't get it to work anymore.

That's how the shed had started. His garden shed. But a garden shed with a difference. In it there was an old easy chair, a small pine table, several bottles of different home-made wines, a small oil stove, a kettle, a cup and saucer and some books. Books that Judith Wright would not have understood. Books that she certainly wouldn't have had in the house. But they were books that allowed Lionel to live a fantasy life. A life that compared with great lovers, like Don Juan and Casanova. And all it needed were the books and the privacy of his shed.

'Won't you try getting up, dear?' Lionel begged his wife. 'Roger's on the mend now. I'm sure he'd like to see you.'

'I can't go near that place again, Lionel. Don't ask me. Not even for Roger.'

And her eyes had filled with tears and she had turned away and buried her head in her pillows. Lionel stayed for five minutes, standing inadequately, looking out over the front garden. He didn't understand.

It was a pity about the baby, but the doctors had said Roger would be fine. And in a day or two both he and Hilary would be home. Lionel put out a hand to touch Judith, but somehow failed to make the necessary contact to comfort her. After a minute longer he turned, went downstairs and out to the shed.

Judith heard him go. She supposed he was going to the garden or that smelly old shed of his. She wondered what he got up to out there. He said he was writing a book and couldn't be interrupted, but sometimes she doubted it. Making her knock before she could go in. And then there was that great big padlock on the door when he was at work. Still, there was no harm in it.

It kept Lionel happy. And it got him out of her way. And that was what she wanted, she told herself. Although it hadn't always been that way. At the beginning she couldn't bear to be away from her Lionel.

Judith shook her head. He didn't understand about Roger and Hilary. And she couldn't explain because it was nothing she could put into words. It was just a feeling, an idea that had come into her head when that horrible sound went round the hospital. It had been like some great beast dying. And somehow, Judith knew that Roger and Hilary's life would never be the same again.

She knew with a mother's closeness that Roger was in danger. She didn't know how, or from what. But she did know that no matter what anyone did, Roger would not, could not, escape.

Judith started to cry again. They'd taken Peter from her, surely that was enough. It had taken her weeks to recover from his death. Months before she'd felt strong enough to get up and go out and about again. Lionel had been very good, then. She wondered how he would manage this time.

It had been Dr Willis who had taken charge of the dead thing. The nurses had refused to touch it. And even Albert Stowell had turned pale and rushed from the theatre as soon as the operation was over. Dr Willis had warned them not to speak to anyone about what had happened. They were to refer all questions to him. He would get rid of the dead foetus and make his report to the hospital authorities. They had been only too willing to leave it to him.

It had been Dr Willis's original intention to examine the

foetus, there and then, but that had proved impossible. Too many people had wanted to know what was going on. And then there was the patient herself. She had needed more attention. He had spoken to the husband's father, Mr Wright. He seemed steady enough, thank God. The mother had gone completely to pieces.

And so the foetus, the thing, had remained unexamined. Dr Willis had taken it down to the Pathology Lab, put it in a solution of formaldehyde and locked it away in his cupboard, safe from prying eyes.

He'd seen the mother and had a chat with her. She didn't seem to remember anything about the operation. All she could remember was the red van coming towards her and then waking up in a hospital bed. He had told her that the baby was dead, but had made no mention of the strange, misshapen form of the thing. Or of the terrible scream it had uttered in its death throes.

She had taken the news well. And talked about being young, and how there was plenty of time for other children. That had been the hard part. Telling her that there wouldn't be any other children. He'd tried to be very gentle with her and explained that her pelvis had got damaged during the birth. He had tried to make it sound normal. It happened from time to time. There was nothing they could do about it. She said she understood and had thanked him for being honest with her.

She had seemed quite calm, almost too calm. Dr Willis had made a note to keep an eye on her. Perhaps the shock had been too much. Perhaps he should have waited until she was stronger before telling her there would be no more children.

But he had felt it kinder to get it over with, rather than let false hopes take hold. He had worried for a while about not being completely honest about the foetus, but after further reflection felt sure he'd done the right thing. Perhaps he would just hint to the father that maybe it was for the best. And he could pass it on if he felt he needed to, or that it would help.

Dr Willis thought about his own son, David. And about Mary, his wife. He had missed them both, every day since they'd died.

Mary most of all. David had only been 4 years old when he'd died and while he was a happy little chap, Dr Willis's hospital work had meant that he really hadn't seen much of him. Until the end.

No, it was Mary he really missed. He remembered their first meeting as if it was yesterday. There was nothing very original about it. It was the same story that a hundred other medical students could tell.

He had been at Guys, in his final year. And Mary had been there too, in her first year, as a nurse. They had met at one of the winter dances, in the nurses' home, and had quickly become inseparable. That was whenever their various duties allowed.

There had never been much question in anyone's mind that Robert Willis and Mary Jardine would get married. And married they had been, six months after that first dance.

Soon after that, Robert had left Guys and gone into partnership with two older doctors in Ashstead in Surrey. That's when they had found the cottage. And Mary had given up work to help him in the practice. Two short years later, David had been born, and Mary had died.

Dr Willis's sister, June, had come to help look after the baby. But neither the cottage nor the practice had been the same without Mary. And after six months, or so, he had sold up and gone into the hospital service.

When David had died a few years later, Robert Willis had sunk himself into his work. And in what free time he let himself have, he read and re-read the many books he had on mythology. A subject he had first become interested in at Cambridge.

But none of it took the place of Mary who he still missed, even after all these years.

Roger had regained consciousness a day and a half after the accident. He felt well enough in himself, but was worried about Hilary. He had asked one of the nurses if she could find out anything, but had been told that Dr Willis would be coming to see him soon.

There were messages from his mother and father, from Susan and Steve, and from the agency. The last one written on a card attached to a bottle of champagne. The nurse had also told him that the police were waiting to talk to him as soon as the doctor said they could.

Roger's mind went back to the night of the accident. He could remember the evening with Steve and Susan. They'd been talking about holidays and the possibility of all four of them going to the Greek Islands next year, if Roger's parents would have the baby. He remembered having a last brandy and Hilary saying to be careful. And getting into the car and starting to drive home to Wimbledon, but after that there was nothing. What had happened? Had it been his fault? Or the other driver's? What about the other driver? What had happened to him? The police were outside: did that mean he was dead?

A tall man with grey hair and prominent features came into the room. Roger supposed it was Dr Willis. The doctor looked at the chart at the end of the bed and then asked, 'How are you feeling today?'

'I'm all right. A bit of a sore head still, but otherwise all right. It's Hilary I'm worried about. Is she . . .' Roger left the question unfinished.

'She's on the mend,' Dr Willis answered him. 'She's just down the corridor a bit. You can go along and see her for yourself tomorrow.'

'Has she had . . . what about the baby?' Roger asked uncertainly.

'I'm afraid he was still-born,' Dr Willis replied, as softly as he could. 'It was all a bit much for her.'

'It was a boy then?' Roger asked.

'Yes. Yes, it would have been a boy.'

'She wanted a boy, particularly. I don't know why. Women usually want girls don't they? Was she very . . . upset?'

Dr Willis turned and looked out of the window. 'She's taken it very well, Mr Wright. Very well indeed. I'm afraid I've had to give her some other bad news. And you too, of course.'

Dr Willis paused as if to allow Roger time to prepare himself. But in truth his eye had been caught by a cat sitting on the roof opposite. It appeared to be staring at him and for some reason Dr Willis found it particularly disturbing. He turned away from the window and back towards his patient.

'What is the other news, Doctor?' Roger prompted.

'I'm afraid that in the course of the accident and the subsequent delivery your wife's pelvis has been damaged. It means, I'm afraid, that your wife won't be able to bear any more children, Mr Wright. I'm sorry.' Roger was silent for a minute. Dr Willis looked over his shoulder, the cat was still there.

'But she's all right apart from that?' Roger asked. 'I mean, she isn't injured or in pain or anything?'

'No. Don't worry yourself on that score. She's perfectly healthy. And you're going to be fine too. You'll both be out of here in a day or two.'

'What about the other driver?' Roger asked, not wanting to hear the answer.

Dr Willis frowned. 'He wasn't so lucky, I'm afraid. His head went through the windscreen with quite a lot of force and his face is quite a mess. Quite a mess. Still, we'll do the best we can for the poor chap. It's a nasty business all round. And I'm afraid it's not over yet. The police are going to want to see you both, you know?'

Roger nodded. 'I can't remember much about it, I'm afraid.'

'No, Mr Wert is in much the same state. Frankly I should think they'll let the matter drop. You've all suffered quite enough.'

Dr Willis tugged at his coat, adjusted his stethoscope and walked towards the door.

'There is one thing . . .' he started to say. And then noticed that the cat was still there. Still staring at him.

'Yes?' Roger prompted, after a minute.

'Yes. I haven't said anything to your wife, but the foetus wasn't quite normal. So although I know it's a hard thing to say, perhaps everything has turned out for the best. Nature has a way you know,' Dr Willis said and opened the door.

'What was wrong with the baby?' Roger asked.

Dr Willis hesitated. 'Let's just say it wasn't quite the right shape, if you see what I mean, Mr Wright, and leave it at that.' And gave Roger no alternative but to leave it at that by the simple act of walking out of the door and closing it firmly behind him.

'Christ all fucking mighty!'

'Mr Wert!'

'I'm sorry, nurse. But it's a bit of a stopper ain' it? I mean, I used to be a good looking bloke, got around a bit, know what I mean? They won't look twice at me now.'

'Of course they will,' Mandy Brown said trying to cheer up the patient. 'It's what's on the inside that counts. You're still the same person. I'm sure if the girls liked you before, they'll still like you. It's a relationship any nice girl's looking for,' she added and thought of her Bob who she hoped was looking for a relationship, too.

Ian Wert didn't say anything. He just sat looking at his face in the mirror. It looked like one of those advertisements on the telly telling you to use your seat belt. What a bloody mess. Relationship? You could stuff them. His lips formed a painful, mouthless grin. That was just what he wasn't going to be doing when they caught a look at his boatrace. It looked like some sort of lace mat his Granny used to make.

'What about the other geezer? What 'appened to 'im?' he asked.

'His wife lost the baby she was carrying.'

'Oh. Done 'imself a favour then, ain't 'e. I mean 'o wants those little bleeders running around all over the place?'

Mandy Brown laughed. 'Well, it may surprise you to know that quite a lot of people do. I'm sure the Wrights did.'

'What happened to 'im?'

'He was unconscious for two days, but he's all right now.'

'You mean that's all? That's all that 'appened to 'im after the way 'e was going all over the road. And I end up like this, like bloody scarface the second?'

Mandy Brown finished dressing his face and stood up. 'I thought you told the police you didn't remember what happened?'

'I don't, but it wasn't my bleeding fault. I know that.'

And Ian Wert knew more. A lot more than he'd told the law. In fact, he remembered very clearly the events leading up to the accident. But he didn't want the filth checking up on him, going around his mates, finding out what he'd been up to that Saturday night. And who knows what else. Once they started, they just went on and on. Better to 'ave nothing to do with them. That's what his dad had taught him. Be polite, but don't know nothing. And this time he had the perfect excuse. There was nothing they could do. Especially as it seemed the other bugger and his missus really couldn't remember anything. Well that's what they said.

But they weren't going to get away with it. Ian didn't

want the law involved, but when he was up and about again he'd have a look at the Wrights and maybe find a way of getting his own back. Ian was not one to forgive, either a real or an imagined hurt, easily.

He started thinking about women and in particular Nurse Brown. He wondered what she would be like. She had good legs but she was a bit flat-chested. Maybe he'd give it a try tomorrow.

In Alpha Foxtrot Two Zero, Jim Scott and Bob Holloway sat comparing notes. They had spoken to all three of the people involved in the accident and the numerous people who turned up after the crash. They'd talked to Susan and Steve Palmer and, although he didn't know it, a couple of Ian Wert's friends, but they still had nothing.

'What do you think?' Jim Scott asked.

'I don't rightly know, Jim. The Wrights seem honest enough folk, I don't think they remember anything. But as for that other little bugger, Wert, he's a right villain he is. It wouldn't surprise me if he's up to all sorts of things on the side. I wouldn't mind half an hour with him in a dark cell somewhere.'

'You think he knows something and isn't saying?'

'It's just a feeling. You know what I mean?'

Jim Scott nodded his blonde head. He knew what his partner meant all right. He had the same sort of feeling himself. He was quite sure that Ian Wert remembered what had happened, and wasn't saying. But he couldn't think why. The position of the cars made it more likely that the Wrights were in the wrong.

'Well?' Bob Holloway asked with a grin. 'What are we going to do?'

'Hand it over to them back at the station. Let them decide. It's what they're bloody paid for.'

'That's the first sensible bloody thing you've said

today. You'll end up coming back to Yorkshire with me if you go on like this.'

Jim Scott laughed and started the car. 'What? End up like you? No thank you. I'd rather be a southern poofta!'

The pathology lab was in the west wing of St Michael's Hospital, on the second floor. Dr Willis had been trying to get there for the last hour. But each time he'd left his office someone had caught him and steered him off in another direction. Would he look at some patient or another or could they ask his opinion on some matter of hospital business? Finally, though, he had made it. He had half an hour to spare and he was going to examine the foetus, the thing from the other night. He had thought about it a lot, over the last two days, discussed it with Stowell and even gone back and done a bit of reading on the subject.

If his theory was right, then he feared that he would not be able to keep it to himself. While wishing to spare the Wrights any pain or embarrassment the cause of medical science had always to be served.

Dr Willis opened the door of the pathology lab. It was empty, as he'd expected it to be at this time. But it was not as he'd expected to find it. The place was a complete mess. It looked as if a storm had gone through it. His eyes went to the cupboard that had housed the foetus. The door was shattered. It was as if some giant fist had smashed its way through the thin wood panelling. The specimen jar that had held the foetus was shattered. The wood and floor near the cupboard were still wet.

Dr Willis shook his head in disbelief. Why should anyone want to do a thing like this? There was nothing here of value. The laboratory was a wreck. Test tubes, jars, dishes, cabinets all had been broken or smashed. It was as if some awful thing had run riot over the bench tops.

Thing? Dr Willis stopped for a moment and thought again, thing! Surely not. The foetus had been dead. He himself had examined it. Had seen and heard it die. And anyway it was too fanciful for words. This was a hospital in 1981, not some gas-lit castle of the late 19th century.

A movement at the window caught his eye. Dr Willis looked up and found himself looking into the biggest pair of emerald green eyes he'd ever seen. They belonged to a black cat that was sitting on the sill of the large, old hospital windows. And they were watching every move he made.

Dr Willis went over to the cupboard. The cat padded along to the next window sill and sat observing him as he hunted with increasing urgency for any trace of the foetus. There was none.

Who? What? Why? Dr Willis didn't know the answers but in his heart of hearts he knew that somehow it was something to do with the cat that was watching him through the window. And he began to be afraid.

Over the next two days there were visits for Hilary and Roger from Susan and Steve and from Roger's father. Roger wished again that Hilary's Aunt Joan were around or that his mother felt stronger. Sue was very sweet but he felt Hilary needed the help of an older woman. She seemed calm enough, perhaps too calm, too detached, too sanguine about what had happened. Roger had expected her to be depressed, even weepy, but she was neither of these things. There was just a quietness that Roger found disturbing.

He had thought that she might change when she got home, but she hadn't. She had picked up her life, as if nothing had happened. She had insisted he go back to work and had told Sue she could manage quite well when her friend had offered to come and stay a few days.

Back in the agency everyone was kindness itself. Ben

Handshore offered them the use of his holiday flat in Majorca. And Robin Edwards, the Creative Director, had told Roger to take off as much time as he needed.

It was only at home that there was a lack of warmth. Hilary did all the things she usually did. And did them in her own conscientious way. The house was spotless. The meals were delicious, but somehow the warmth seemed to have gone, temporarily Roger hoped, from their marriage. She no longer came over to him and gave him the little kisses and hugs that had been so much part of their relationship since they'd met five years ago.

He had fallen in love right from the start with Hilary's black hair and green eyes, and her long, lithe figure. But more than anything else, it was her sweet nature, her natural kindness that made him certain that this was the only girl for him.

And to his delight he had found that she felt the same way about him. And they had made a handsome couple. Roger with his tall good looks and blonde curly hair and beard and blue eyes. Hilary only an inch or two shorter, like some latter-day Cleopatra.

Everything had seemed to go right from the start, Roger had got a good job at JOY Advertising. And their combined salaries had been more than enough to pay the mortgage on the old Victorian house they'd seen in Waverly Road. There had only been the question of a deposit and that had been taken care of by some money left to Hilary by her parents, and kept in trust for her by Aunt Joan.

Over the next four years they'd worked hard at the house and it was now worth twice what they'd paid for it. And there was plenty of room to expand. There were four bedrooms, Roger's den, a lounge, a dining room, a bathroom and a downstairs toilet and a big kitchen. And if that wasn't enough there was always the cellar.

Then last Christmas they had made the decision to start

a family, and almost immediately Hilary became pregnant. And no-one doubted that the child of such a handsome and happy couple would be anything but perfect. Because in everyone's opinion the Wrights had got it made.

That was until the night of the accident.

Chapter Four

The storm came at night, late at night, but it had been threatening all day. It had been heavy and close when Roger and Hilary had woken up. They had niggled at each other in the bathroom and over coffee and toast. And the argument had finally flared up when Roger had said he was going to see his mother on the way home.

'Is she still playing the invalid?' Hilary asked with uncharacteristic spitefulness. 'Anyone would think it was she who had lost the baby.'

'Oh come on, Hilary, be fair. She's upset about you and me, as well as the baby.'

'About you, you mean. Her precious son. That's all she cares about.'

'That's a cheap bloody remark. What's got into you today?'

Hilary looked at the hurt in Roger's eyes.

'I'm sorry, Roger. I didn't mean it. It's the weather, and . . . everything.'

'Are you sure you wouldn't like to go away? We could take up Ben's offer to use his flat in Majorca.'

Hilary shook her head.

'No, really, I'll be all right, Roger. I don't think being away will help.'

Roger looked at his watch.

'God! I've got to get going. There's a meeting at 9.30 on Kleen-Ade.'

He gulped the last of his coffee, picked up his briefcase, kissed Hilary on the forehead and made for the door. At the door he paused for a minute before going out.

'Are you sure you're all right?' he asked again.

'Sure,' Hilary said and blew him a kiss.

But she wasn't sure. Hilary sat at the breakfast table for a long time after Roger had left. She knew that she had changed since the accident. She felt more independent, not only of Roger, but of everyone around. And she knew that she'd become more critical, sharper. One or two of the things she'd heard herself say shocked her. They were spiteful and, what was more, while she was sorry after she'd said them, at the time she quite enjoyed the hurt the remark had caused.

And then there was the loss of the baby. Their baby. The one that she and Roger had planned and had been so looking forward to. Hilary knew that she should be more upset about the loss of the baby. But she couldn't be. Somehow she felt it would be all right in the end. Dr Willis had said that she wouldn't be able to have any more children after the miscarriage, but somewhere deep within her, something seemed to be telling her that everything would be all right.

And there was one other thing. Perhaps the most strange of all. Her body was beginning to feel different. She could not explain it except that it felt tauter, leaner, more supple. The doctor had told her to take it easy but she found herself constantly on the move, stretching, flexing herself. And then, suddenly, the feeling was over and she would relax completely and fall asleep for an hour at a time.

Hilary got up from the kitchen table and told herself not to be silly. She would ring up Sue and suggest they have a cup of coffee. There was nothing wrong with her that some hard work and the company of some friends wouldn't cure.

Hilary Wright wasn't the only one who lingered over her breakfast. Dr Willis too had plenty to occupy his thoughts. For a start there was his dream. A dream that had found him in a strange world full of cats. In the beginning they had ignored him. But then one or two had expressed a mild curiosity. He had sensed no antagonism, at first. Indeed some of them had seemed quite friendly. But later the mood had changed. They had become suspicious. They had been led by a slim, black and white cat with patches of grey. The markings were quite unusual, the black on the face being edged perfectly with white, giving the impression that the cat was wearing a mask.

He had not understood what they were saying, but he knew they were talking and that they were talking about him. The cat with the mask-like face had had a lot to say. Dr Willis had felt them all turn towards him. A wicked-looking Siamese, a grey Persian, a Burmese fighting-cat. And then had come the evil-looking black cat with the big green eyes. It was just like the one Dr Willis imagined was observing him from the hospital roof.

They had started to move towards him. They were like the big cats of the jungle. Their movements were silent and stealthy. Dr Willis remembered, he had turned to run, but there were more of the animals behind him. And then the first one, the big black one, had sprung, his claws ripping deep into Dr Willis's flesh. The others had followed and Dr Willis had woken crying out in agony and bathed in perspiration. He had not been able to get back to sleep.

Dr Willis looked out of the kitchen window. There were two cats in the garden. One of them belonged to next door, but the other was the one he'd seen on the hospital roof. And in his dream. It was the black one with the big green eyes.

The doctor turned away from the window and poured himself another cup of tea. This time he put two spoonfuls of sugar in the cup. Hot sweet liquid was what he needed to comfort him. All of his training as a man of medicine, a man of science, told him that what he was imagining was impossible. But he kept coming back to the foetus, the thing that looked as if it was half-human, half-animal. Half-cat!

And what had happened to it? Where had it gone? Who would have taken it? Why would anyone damage the pathology laboratory? Why did he feel he was being watched, followed, by this black cat with green eyes? Question after question that he had no sensible answer for bombarded Dr Willis's tired brain.

There was only one answer, however inexplicable, however fantastic it might seem. The thing had a life of its own. It had not been dead despite everything his training and knowledge told him. The foetus had been alive, or more fantastically still, had come alive again. And it had forced its way out of the cupboard and the laboratory. Everything about the damage to the cupboard pointed to that explanation. The wood had splintered from the inside. The marks on the inside of the door resembled claw marks. The damage to the equipment was such as might have been caused by the sweeping motion of a powerful, clawed animal.

And Dr Willis knew that the limb belonged to something that was angry. Angry with him. And that the thing was planning to take revenge. Dr Willis's hand shook as he put the cup back in its saucer. He was afraid. He went through into the surgery, opened the drug cupboard and took a double dose of valium to soothe his nerves.

But he knew that any relief would only be temporary. He was sure the nightmare would come back. And that the black cat would not go away until it had taken its revenge.

Carol Coren had surprised herself with some of the things she'd managed to do in the last five or six days. First, of course, there was the decision to leave home. And then there was the return trip to get the money and the fight with Bill. But there was more. She had found out Hilary's name and address. She had even got herself a room round the corner from Waverly Road. And then, for the first time in her life, she had got a job. True, it wasn't a very brilliant job, but it paid £40 a week, and that was more than Carol had ever been given as a regular sum.

Her housekeeping from Bill had had to be fought for, day by day. And there had been times when he had forced her to earn the money she needed to buy clothes, by making her do extra things, things like he'd tried to make her do on that last night, during the day when he came home for lunch.

Today was her second day at the Lemon Tree Coffee Shop. They'd seemed quite pleased with her yesterday, although she'd never done anything like it before.

The bell on the shop door rang and Carol looked up. It was Hilary Wright. Carol nodded to the other waitress. 'I'll get it.'

'Please yourself,' Maureen answered and went back to thinking about how she could get Mick Bennett away from Sheilah Askey.

'Coffee, please,' Hilary said, looking up from her shopping list.

'White or black, please?'

'Black.'

'Anything to eat?' Carol asked and just managed to stop herself enquiring how Hilary was feeling.

'No thank you,' Hilary replied and looked a little more intently at the small, slightly greying woman in the brown overall. Carol went back towards the kitchen and Hilary followed her with her eyes. There was something strangely familiar about the thin, eager to please face. But Hilary was sure that it hadn't been in here, the Lemon Tree Coffee Shop, that she had first seen the face.

Carol came back with the coffee.

'Will there be anything else?' she asked.

'No, thank you.'

Carol started to walk away.

'Have you worked here long?' Hilary called after her.

Carol turned.

'No, I only started yesterday.'

Hilary shook her head.

'I'm sorry, I thought we'd met before,' she said tentatively.

'We have, Mrs Wright. I used to live near where you had your accident. I was the first one there when it happened. I spoke to you when they were getting you out of the car and over to the ambulance.'

Hilary remembered the woman walking beside her, comforting her. And, for the first time, she remembered something else too. The voice that had seemed to speak to her inside her head.

'You were very kind, thank you,' she said to the woman.

Carol smiled with pleasure. She wasn't used to people thanking her. And now, two days running someone had appreciated something she'd done.

An older couple came into the shop and Carol moved to serve them. Hilary sipped her coffee, thoughtfully. She felt strangely concerned about the woman. She seemed so vulnerable and so eager to please. The manageress came out of a small door at the back of the coffee shop and switched the lights on. Hilary looked outside and realised that it had got very dark.

It was still only 11.30. There was going to be a storm, she thought, and for some reason felt excited at the prospect. She paid her bill and stopped for a word with Carol.

'Do you live near here now?' she asked.

'Yes, Mrs Wright. Just round the corner from you.'

'Perhaps we'll see each other again, then,' Hilary said, and discovered she wasn't at all surprised to find that the woman knew where she lived.

For her part, Carol Coren was sure they would see each

other again. Last night had made that certain. Because Carol had finally remembered why Hilary Wright's face had seemed so familiar.

It had suddenly come to her. It had been a long time ago, but the place she'd seen Hilary Wright before was her own village.

And there was something else. It had taken Carol a while to sort it all out in her memory. But slowly the pieces had fallen into place. It was something her mother had told her. A story that had gone round the village about little Hilary Robinson's birth.

It had been at the time of the full moon. At midnight. And the story was that at the precise moment Hilary was born, all the animals in the village had gone slightly mad.

Dogs and cats that had lain asleep, woke and barked and meowed. Cows and sheep in the fields joined in the chorus and the air was suddenly sweet with the song of birds.

It was as if the animal world was rejoicing. But there had been tragedy too. For in giving birth to Hilary, Mrs Robinson had died. And six weeks later, Mr Robinson had been killed in a car crash.

Hilary had gone to live with an aunt. But Carol remembered her coming back to the village to visit her parents' grave. And to see the house where she was born.

The village. That was a link. And Carol was sure that it was not one that was about to be broken.

Outside the air was heavy and oppressive. People made jokes about the end of the world. In offices and shops lights were switched on and windows opened to catch the slightest whisper of a breeze. Mistakes were made, bosses blamed their subordinates who in turn snapped at their juniors.

There was everywhere an electricity in the air that seemed to promote a kind of madness. In a big London store a middle-aged woman took off all her clothes and sprayed herself with scent taken from the perfume counter. On the underground a young man started singing hymns at the top of his voice and was beaten, nearly to death, by his fellow passengers. There were other things too. Nasty evil things. Like the things Dominic Hughes and Ronald Shelton did to Mrs Watt's baby.

Both boys were 11 years old, both lived in Shillingford Street and both should have been at St Joseph's School. But today, both boys had decided to stay away from school. It was not something they had ever done before, or that they would be in a position to do ever again.

Dominic Hughes had one pound fifty on him. Fifty pence of that was his lunch money. The other pound he had stolen from his mother's purse. And that was something he had never done before. Ronnie Shelton had his sandwiches and twenty pence he'd taken from the kitchen table while his elder sister's back had been turned.

At first the two boys had been content to wander around the streets and shops, hiding in doorways when they saw someone who might recognize them. They had bought themselves a couple of cokes and a cream bun and eaten them at the bus station as they watched the buses come in and out.

They had gone into Woolworths and dared each other to steal as much as they could without getting caught. Dominic had won. After that Ronald had suggested putting rubbish through everyone's letter boxes. And then suddenly there had been Mrs Watt's baby, Jane, in her pram in Mrs Watt's front garden.

They had started by taking baby Jane for a walk, in her pram. They had gone up Frith Street and turned left by the waste ground near the old canal. It was Dominic who suggested that it would be fun to see if baby Jane could walk. She couldn't. But she could crawl. And so they made her crawl over the rough, rubble-littered ground. Soon her tiny little hands and knees were bleeding profusely from the many small cuts and grazes that had laid her flesh bare.

Still Dominic and Ronald forced her on, even though her cries grew louder and louder. Ronald had found a solution to that. He had removed the child's, now heavily soiled nappy, and stuffed it in its mouth. Not to be outdone, Dominic pointed to a small hill of rubbish that led to a bed of nettles. Soon baby Jane was rolling down the hill. The nettles whipped at her shredded flesh inflicting fresh pains on the small battered body. The tiny arms and legs tried to claw their way out of the bed of pain, but each time she managed to get herself to the edge of the nettles, one of the two small boys was there to kick her back in again.

Soon the small child lay still. Its body was a mass of blood, dirt and excrement. The nappy had come out of its mouth, but it made no sound. The two boys picked up the small figure and put it back in the pram. They covered it with a blanket and pushed the pram back to Mrs Watt's house and left it in her garden, before going home for tea.

They didn't really know what they had done. And they certainly didn't know why they had done it. But then it was a funny kind of day. Hot and sticky, it made you feel strange. That's all they could tell the police when eventually they came to call.

Dominic and Ronald weren't the only ones who found the day funny, or found themselves doing strange, even evil things. The police were inundated with calls reporting cold-blooded crimes of violence completely outside the normal number or pattern. It was the kind of day when the seemingly impossible, almost unbelievable, happened with abnormal regularity.

The fire brigade, hospitals, doctors, and a hundred other emergency services received calls that strained their resources, their skills and their patience to the utmost.

In Balham, a barber cut the ears off a customer he was

shaving and then cut his own throat. In Manchester, a keeper at the Bellvue Zoo turned loose all the animals and caused panic and death in the streets of that city.

Dogs turned on owners, old women wise in the ways of the country uttered and muttered strange oaths and told strange stories.

The death toll on the road was double that of a normal day. And the number of accidents in the home were beyond count.

In comparison to all of this, Roger Wright's day was an oasis of calm. There had been the row with Hilary in the morning and certainly the Kleen-Ade meeting had been difficult. The agency had disagreed amongst themselves and the client had disagreed with everyone. The work that Roger and Steve had done had been thrown out and they had been asked to start again. Roger was more upset by the decision than Steve.

'It happens, Roger, you know that. It's a rotten day and the client's in a rotten mood. His wife probably didn't give it to him last night. It happens all the time. It's the business. Anyway you can hardly blame him. We weren't one agency, indivisible, as the man said.'

'Well they can get someone else to write the next campaign,' Roger threatened. 'I've had enough.'

'Come on, Rog, everyone knows you've had a bellyful recently, but we've had this situation plenty of times before and sorted it out. How's Hilary?'

Roger made a face.

'All right.'

'But different?' Steve suggested.

'Yes. Yes, that's right. I can't explain it, not properly, anyway. She's just different. I keep putting it down to losing the baby, but I don't know, Steve.'

'I wasn't going to say anything, but Sue and I were talking last night. She feels the same way. On the surface Hilary is the same old Hilary she's always been, but underneath, she's different. For a start she doesn't seem to want to see anyone very much. Susan's rung her a dozen times, but most of the time Hilary says she's busy.'

Roger put his feet up on his desk and knocked a cup of coffee over some freshly typed copy.

'Shit!' he shouted savagely.

When the two of them had finished mopping up, Steve said, 'Why don't you and Hilary come over to dinner one night soon. Maybe if we all get together we can help get her sorted out.'

'Thanks, Steve. I'd like that. In the meantime I'm going to ask old Doctor Speer to come and see Hils. Maybe there's something he can suggest.'

Ian Wert had been home two days. Two long days that had been spent inside his parents' house. His mother, when she was home from the general cleaning job she did, fussed over him. His father, when he was home from the dogtrack or the pub, ignored him and told him he was a fool.

In between times Ian Wert contented himself listening to his collection of jazz records. Several of his mates dropped in bringing beer and cigarettes. And each time Ian had told the story of the crash. Each time altering it a little, adding a detail, remembering a fact that didn't always exist to be remembered.

And each time, as he told the story, his determination to take his revenge grew stronger. He didn't know what he would do yet, or how, or when he would do it. But he knew that he wasn't going to let the Wrights get away with what they'd done to him. Each time he looked in the mirror at the bright, pink, shiny network of scars on his face he invented some new torture.

But what Ian Wert wanted most was a woman. It had been ten days. It was the longest time he'd ever been without a woman since he was fourteen. As he sat alone in his parents' small house his mind ran through the list of girls he knew, or had known. He didn't want sympathy. More than anything else he wanted to be accepted as himself. As he was before the accident.

Ian looked at his watch. It was the middle of the day. It wasn't a question of who, but of who was around. If Pat Wilkins was still working at the shoe factory, she'd be home for lunch. Just. He picked up the phone he'd persuaded his parents to install, and that he'd paid for, and dialled the number.

Pat answered, Ian started on a line of chat he'd practiced over the years. But this time with a few variations. Yes, she'd heard he'd been in an accident. And that he'd hurt his face, but it wasn't his face she was interested in, she said with a giggle.

'Do you feel like coming round to see me?' Ian asked.

'When?'

'Now. This afternoon!'

'I'm due back at 2 o'clock.'

'You could always be ill.'

Pat thought about it. She hadn't seen Ian for a while. And he was good to a girl, as long as she gave out. 'O.K. But I'll have to think of something to tell mum. And I'll have to have me dinner,' Pat whispered.

'I'll get us a drink ready.'

'See you.'

'Yeh,' Ian said and hoped it wouldn't be too much of a shock.

Judith Wright spent most of the morning crying. But also in a state of excitement. The crying was not new. But this feeling of excitement was. And it was the feeling of excitement that got her out of bed and dressed for the first time since the accident.

And more. Judith Wright didn't just get dressed. She took time and care, not only choosing what to wear, but in making up and in doing her hair. Because this feeling, this excitement made her want to look good. It was as if she was young again. It was how she'd felt when she was getting ready to meet Lionel.

It was a feeling of sexual excitement that Judith hadn't felt so urgently, so openly, for a long while.

It was a feeling that Judith liked. Wanted more of. Wanted to do something about. That was when the idea first came to her. The shed. Although Judith had never hinted by word or look that she knew, or was even interested in anything about the shed, she did know that Lionel kept the spare key of the padlock under a paint tin in the garage.

Having the idea, getting the key and walking down the narrow plot of garden to the shed took no time at all. There was a moment of doubt at the door, but it was only a moment. And then Judith was inside the shed. Lionel's shed. The shed that he spent so much time in, the shed that had almost seemed to come between them in the last few years.

The first thing that struck Judith, was the smell. There was a mustiness, because the door and windows were tight shut so much of the time. But there was a sweetness as well. And then there was the fruitiness of the home-made wine. It made the atmosphere heavy, sensuous. Judith found it exciting.

She went over to the pine table and looked at the papers that were piled neatly to one side of it. They were covered in Lionel's handwriting. She was surprised. She had never believed the book-writing story. Perhaps she would have a little peek at it later, but in the mean time there were other things.

A small, rather oriental cupboard to the right of the door took Judith's eye. It contained a little oriental teapot, a teacup to match and several blends of heavily scented tea. On the upper shelf there was a packet of joss sticks and two packets of Gossamer Durex. Judith was shocked but she was also intrigued.

She closed the cupboard and moved over to a book shelf that Lionel had built along one whole side of the shed. She took down one of the books and let it fall open. The words seemed to leap off the page at her. Never in her life had Judith read such indescribable filth. But she could not stop reading. Or looking at the pictures that had started by making her gasp, but were rapidly having a different effect altogether.

Judith forced herself to put the book down and continue her examination of the shed. There were more books, like the first, or worse. There were magazines. And there were gadgets. And in Lionel's old school tuck box there was an inflatable plastic doll that had blonde hair and a set of black underwear.

Judith sat down in the armchair. Her mind in a turmoil. To find out, after all these years that Lionel had such – such appetites, well it wasn't the Lionel she knew. She and Lionel had always enjoyed such straight sex. She put her hand to her head and her elbow touched the paper on the pine table. Lionel's book. She'd forgotten it amongst all the other discoveries. Judith turned to pick up the papers. There wasn't any doubt in her mind what kind of book it would be.

She turned to page one and started reading. As she read she grew more and more excited. Lionel had written this. She moved her legs slightly apart on the chair. And then together again. It was a pleasant sensation, and Judith made the movement again, several times until her breathing quickened and she felt a wetness between her legs. It helped a little. But she knew it would only do until Lionel got home. Because by now Judith had already decided that when her husband got home from work that evening, she would be waiting for him.

Was that why she'd taken so much trouble with her

appearance? Was that the excitement she'd felt when she'd woken up? What was happening to her? Judith didn't understand, but she had the feeling, the ridiculous feeling, that it was somehow connected to the accident.

Chapter Five

Mrs Tressel had lived at number 31 Warpole Road for over fifty years. And for the last ten years, Timothy had lived with her. Every day, twice a day, Mrs Tressel and Timothy went for a walk together. And as they walked, stopping every now and then, Mrs Tressel talked to Timothy and told him what she thought of the world and what was happening to it.

Timothy didn't say much. He just sniffed, and grunted and sometimes growled. Because Timothy was a corgi and he was nearly as old as Mrs Tressel. Mrs Tressel was 79 and Timothy was 13.

They shared other features in common too. They were both short in the leg. Both a little deaf and their eyesight was beginning to fade rather fast. But they managed. And the people of Wilner's Green knew them, and watched for them and gave a friendly greeting whenever they went past.

It was true that Timothy did have the habit of leaving little presents where they weren't always wanted, but the dog was such a sweet old thing, and his mistress such a nice old lady, that no-one really minded. In her time Mrs Tressel had done plenty of people in Wilner's Green a kindness or two.

Recently Mrs Tressel had wondered how much longer she and Timothy could go on. She got very tired these days. And Timothy had got slower and slower on his walks since his left back leg became a little swollen.

Mrs Tressel did not mention this to Timothy as they prepared to go for their evening walk. But the feeling was particularly strong today. It was a funny kind of day.

Heavy and depressing. Timothy could feel the electricity in the air, too. Mrs Tressel could tell he was uneasy and nervous. She was sure there was a storm on the way.

'Come on, TT,' she urged, using her pet name for the overweight corgi. Timothy didn't move. Mrs Tressel bent low and snapped the lead onto his collar. 'Come on, old chap, walkies.' She gave a tug at the lead, but Timothy's rear quarters remained planted firmly on the ground.

Mrs Tressel tugged at the lead again. Timothy made a low growling noise in his throat, but he still didn't move. Mrs Tressel pulled harder.

'Now come along, Timothy Tressel,' she said sharply. 'Please,' she added despairingly after a minute.

Something in his mistress's tone got to the old dog, and reluctantly he got to his feet and followed her unwillingly to the front door.

'That's better,' Mrs Tressel encouraged. 'We won't be long, but we're both getting older and we need our exercise. It's going to rain later and you won't want to go out then, will you?'

Mrs Tressel shut the front door behind her, double-locking it, as the insurance man had impressed on her to do. He had also told her to lock the windows, even the small ones, but Mrs Tressel did not think it was necessary when they were only going to be gone some fifteen minutes or so.

Outside it had got darker. The air was still and quiet with menace. A solitary bird sang a sharp, shrill note of warning. Timothy wandered warily along the well-trodden path of their evening walk. The faithful old dog knew something was wrong.

Mrs Tressel felt something was wrong too. The road was deserted. And despite the appalling gloom most of the houses were in darkness. There were no friendly greetings today. Mrs Tressel shivered despite the thundery heat. Timothy went about his business in various gardens and paths along the road.

They turned the corner into Hogarth Gardens. At number 7 Mr Dixon was working in his front garden. Timothy trotted up to him and sniffed at his feet. He knew Mr Dixon liked him. Two yards down the street Mrs Tressel heaved a sigh of relief that something was as it should be on this extraordinary day.

Mr Dixon looked at the dog as it came through his front gate. Bloody thing! Always sniffing around his garden. Lifting his leg everywhere. And worse. Well he wasn't going to put up with it any more. He'd give the bloody dog something to remember him by.

He lifted his heavy gardening boot and kicked hard into Timothy's stomach. Timothy yelped with pain and then turned snarling at Mr Dixon. He lunged at Mr Dixon's ankle and bit through the dirt-encrusted trouser and sock into warm flesh. Blood started to run down into Mr Dixon's boot. In a fury he picked up the rake he'd been using and lashed out at the dog. The teeth of the rake bit into Timothy's bad leg, tearing at the flesh as Mr Dixon pulled the tool back ready to strike again.

It had taken Mrs Tressel a minute or two to realize what was happening, but when she did she was quick to react despite her age. So by the time Mr Dixon was ready to take his second swing at Timothy with the rake, he found himself in danger of hitting Mrs Tressel instead of the dog.

Maybe it was the sight of the old lady in front of him, shouting at him through her tears, that cleared his head and made him realise what he'd done. Or, maybe, the inexplicable moment of madness, so foreign to Mr Dixon's nature, just simply passed. But pass it did. Suddenly, and it left Mr Dixon ashamed and at a loss for words.

Timothy cowered by the fence. Mr Dixon started over towards him intent on helping the animal to his feet. But the dog would have none of it. The top lip curled and the animal snarled a warning.

Mrs Tressel went over to Timothy and looked at his leg. The wound was bad. Flesh hung loose in strips from the dog's thigh. And the holes opened by the teeth of the rake were bleeding profusely. Mrs Tressel took out her handkerchief and dabbed gently at the bloody mess. The dog whimpered, pathetically.

Mr Dixon offered to help but neither Mrs Tressel nor Timothy would have any of it. In a super-human effort Mrs Tressel managed to pick the dog up and start the long walk back to her house.

On the way she passed several people she knew, but no-one offered to help. It was that kind of day. And it was getting worse.

It was with relief that Mrs Tressel turned into the pathway of her own house. Her arms and legs were tired from carrying Timothy. Her dress was covered in blood and her eyes were filled by tears of sadness and of anger. She put her foot up to where she knew the step to be and put it down again.

The step was there, but so was something else and Mrs Tressel's foot slipped forward in the dark brown, sticky mess. Her left knee hit the edge of the step and pitched her forward on to her face, dropping Timothy in the process. The wounded animal let out a howl of pain as he hit the paved pathway.

Mrs Tressel looked up from where she lay and saw that the whole of the path was covered in animal droppings of various kinds. Her front door seemed to have some kind of crude messages daubed on it. 'Our gardens are not dogs' shit houses!'

Mrs Tressel staggered to her feet and went over to Timothy. She was too tired and too weak to pick him up again, but she managed to coax him slowly along the path. His wounded leg hung uselessly behind him and he whimpered pitifully all the way to the front door. The old lady dug into her bag for the key. All she wanted to do now was to get inside her house again. They would be safe there. And then she could telephone for help for Timothy. She unlocked the door and pushed it open so that the wounded animal could crawl inside.

But there was to be no sanctuary. There was more muck on the hall carpet. And on the walls. Mrs Tressel gave a cry and followed the filthy smelling trail through to the lounge and the few precious possessions that she had managed to hang on to.

The muck and the filth were everywhere. Every conceivable kind of obscenity had been written or illustrated on the walls. Her pictures, photographs of those once dear to her, the windows, were smeared with excrement.

Mrs Tressel looked around the room. The sight of what she saw was too much for her. The hurt seemed to enter through her head, numbing her mind with the horror of it all. Another, more urgent pain travelled through her. It was her heart. She gasped and called out to Timothy. But the animal couldn't come. He lay in agony by the front door yelping as each new wave of pain seared through his leg.

In the next hour both Mrs Tressel and Timothy were dead. Mrs Tressel very quickly, Timothy more slowly. Later there was to be an investigation, an inquest and a public outcry. No-one could believe the horror of what had happened to the sweet old lady and her dog. But it was that kind of day. It was as if the country had gone mad. A strange day on which strange things happened, altering people's lives in a way that no-one could have foreseen.

Ian Wert lay on the bed watching Pat Wilkins dress. Not that she had many clothes to put on. He grinned. Christ he'd given her a seeing to. Today hadn't turned out so bad, after all.

''Ow do you feel?'

'Sore.'

'You complaining?' he demanded.

She looked over at him. 'Silly.'

'Watcha doin' this evening?'

'Not a lot. Why?'

'Fancy goin' somewhere? Down the pub and then on for a Chinese?'

'That'd be nice.'

Ian thought for a minute. 'I'll meet you at 7 on the corner by the White Lion. All right?'

'All right. See you,' she said and walked out of the bedroom and down the stairs. A minute later, Ian heard the front door go.

He lit a cigarette and lay on the bed thinking about the afternoon. He grinned at the memory of what he'd done, and started to sing. Christ, he'd been good. The way she'd cried out, the whole fucking road must of heard her. That'd show 'em. Whatever else they could say about Ian Wert, there was one thing he could do better than any of 'em. He knew how to give it to a woman.

Ian got off the bed and went into the tiny bathroom. Christ it was hot! He started to run a bath and then went back into the bedroom to clean up a bit before his mum came home. In the distance he could hear a noise that sounded like thunder. He looked out of the window hoping it wasn't going to piss down all night. He'd been planning to give Pat another stuffing down on the tow-path.

At that instant, the first flash of lightning lit up the ever darkening sky. And the pain slashed its way across Ian's face. It was as if the electricity in the air was in some way wired to the network of bright pink scars that covered Ian's face.

The scream went on forever, filling the small house. Ian pressed his face to the pillow and prayed that the pain would go away. Slowly, very slowly, it began to fade.

He sat up on the bed, sweating and shaking, his face still contorted with the memory of the pain. He heard another roll of thunder and shrank back against the wall. Please God, don't let the lightning come again!

He remembered the bath and ran into the bathroom just in time to stop it overflowing. Maybe a bath would calm him down, stop him shaking. He got in and let the warm water close over his lower body.

A breath of wind rattled the window pane. Rain started to drum on the roof. A second flash of lightning arced through the sky. And Ian Wert screamed in torment. He held his head in his hands, pushing hard against his skin desperately trying to blot out the red-hot, searing current that seemed to race around his face. He was sure his cheeks were on fire. Burning. Fucking Jesus, what was happening? Why wouldn't the pain go away?

And then slowly, as before, it did. He opened his eyes in relief, and looked round the bathroom. Everything was as it should be. Ian took a deep breath and let his head sink forward on to his chest.

Plink! Plink! Plink! Three little pools of crimson dropped into the bath turning the water pink around his knees. Perhaps he'd cut himself. Ian looked at his hands, they were clean. He straightened his head and more blood splashed down on to his chest. His hands flew to his face. Christ, one of those fucking scars must have opened up again.

Ian got out of the bath and forced himself to look in the mirror above the sink. The newly formed tissue was intact. But the scars were oozing with blood! As he watched, blood started to run down his face, filling his eyes and then finding its way into the corner of his mouth.

Memories of the accident came back to him. Memories of pain. And then the memories seemed to become reality again. 'No!' he screamed at the mirror and flung his hand and arm over his face. The noises of the crash seemed to roll over him and throw him to the floor, where his mother found him an hour later.

The doctor had no explanation to offer. He was tired and Ian Wert's was not the first strange case he had been called to that day. He gave the young man a strong sedative and prescribed plenty of bed rest. He said he'd call again in a couple of days.

Roger Wright drove home slowly. He hadn't been too keen to get into a car again, but everyone had said the longer you put it off the harder it was. And anyway the agency had been kind and insisted on hiring a car for him until the new one arrived. This was his first longish drive. The heavy rain didn't exactly help and the traffic was bad. He tried to concentrate, but his mind kept going back to the visit he'd just paid to his mother.

He had never seen her like it before. She had looked flushed and excited but had been full of dark warnings and hints that he was in danger. She had cried when he'd left, but had seemed eager for him to go before his father got home from work. Roger had tried to question her several times during the hour-long visit but he could get no further than an unshakeable belief that he was in danger. She did not know why or how, or who from. But it was something to do with the accident. And it was evil.

At first Roger had doubted his mother's sanity. And he was still determined to have a word with his father and suggest she see a doctor of some kind. But so strong was her belief that towards the end of his visit and now, driving back alone in the car, Roger found himself beginning to believe there was something in what she said.

Things had been very strange since the accident. And he had noticed the attitude of people in the hospital towards him had been different. It was almost as if they pitied him. And then there had been Dr Willis's statement that perhaps the baby's death had been for the best. The hint that everything was not quite right.

There was Hilary's behaviour since she'd been home too. She had changed. And Roger knew that it was a deeper change than could be explained by depression caused by the loss of the baby. There was distance between them where before they had always been so very close. In the old days he had known what Hilary was thinking most of the time, but now she was like a closed book to him.

Roger realized the traffic in front of him had stopped and stamped on the brake just in time. He really must pay more attention or there'd be a second accident. He turned on the radio to cheer himself up. Perhaps he was imagining things. It had been a funny day all together.

Lionel Wright opened the front door, called up the stairs to his wife and went into the kitchen to pour himself a drink. He wondered if Roger's visit had helped, had made any difference to her. He took his whisky over to the tap and added some cold water. There were two cups and saucers in the washing-up bowl. Roger must have left them there unless Judith had got up. He realized that Judith had not answered his call when he came in.

Lionel put down his whisky on top of the fridge and went upstairs to the bedroom. It was empty. The room had been tidied and the bed made. Lionel went through to the bathroom and then the spare room. He checked the lavatory. They were all empty. He went downstairs again, this time to the lounge and dining room. There was no sign of Judith. He wondered where she had got to. Perhaps there was a note in the kitchen that he'd missed.

There wasn't. He picked up his drink and took a large swig at it. It was too early to ring Roger, he wouldn't be home yet. Lionel's attention was caught by a movement in the garden. He went over to the back door and peered out into the gloom. There was no-one there. He started to turn away and then stopped, abruptly, as the movement happened again. It was by the shed. His shed! The door was open and banging to and fro in the wind.

Lionel put down his drink, opened the back door and hurried across the lawn. As he drew near he saw the shed light was on. Who the hell was playing about in there. And how had they got in? He pulled open the door and stopped short in his tracks.

It was Judith. But Judith as he had never seen her before. Or, certainly not recently. Her hair was loose and flowing. Her face was expertly made-up, a bright slash of red across the mouth highlighting her full and generous lips. She was half-sitting on his pine table, her legs apart and her breasts stuck out. She was breathing heavily. Her nipples were hard and excited beneath the flimsy black bra that the plastic doll had worn. Her left hand was tucked down the top of the matching panties. And in her right hand was a length of bamboo cane. Her voice was low and husky. 'Come in, Lionel, and shut the door. You've been a very naughty boy, I'm afraid. And I'm going to have to punish you.'

Chapter Six

Roger got home at eight o'clock. He felt terrible after the visit to his mother and then the drive home. He'd hoped that Hilary would be warm and comforting. But she wasn't. She was restless and irritable. They had a makeshift meal on their laps in front of the television. Hilary asked after his mother, but Roger sensed that she was not really interested in the reply.

'Do you want a drink?' Roger asked when they'd finished eating.

'No. I'm going to potter. I can't settle this evening.'

Roger stood up and put his arms round her.

'What's the matter, Hilary?'

She shrugged herself free and turned away from him.

'Nothing. I told you. I'm just restless. It's the weather. Funny things have been happening all day. It was on the news.'

'You can say that again,' Roger said darkly. But she wasn't listening.

Roger poured himself a large whisky and tried to watch television, but it was difficult with Hilary prowling round the room.

'Can't you prowl somewhere else?' Roger snapped and got up to pour himself another drink.

'Haven't you had enough to drink?' Hilary asked and left the room in a huff.

Roger went back to his armchair. He could hear Hilary wandering from room to room, but gradually his attention was captured by a play that had just started on television and he soon forgot all about her.

Hilary knew she hadn't been very nice to Roger, but she

couldn't help it. She wasn't interested in his mother. Or, she realized with a shock, Roger.

It was not because of the baby. Or because she blamed him for the accident. He shouldn't have had that last drink, but he hadn't been drunk. And anyway, Roger was a good driver: Hilary always felt safe with him.

No, the feeling she had was just one of disinterest. And she could sense it getting stronger day by day.

She didn't feel she had to, or wanted to, rely on Roger as she'd used to. And more, she was actually becoming resentful of his interest when he tried to help her.

Hilary walked round the house going first into one room and then into another without being able to settle. She looked out of the bedroom window. It was raining quite hard. Pity, she fancied going for a walk. Hilary sat on the bed and tried to think of something that would release the tension that seemed to be building up in her body. She picked up a book and started to read, but the words just didn't seem to sink in.

Abruptly she closed the book with a snap, got off the bed and left the room. She was going out. Rain or no rain. She took her raincoat out of the downstairs closet and put her head round the living room door.

'I'm going for a walk. See you later,' she said.

Roger looked up from the television in time to see the door close.

'See you,' he muttered and then got up and poured himself another drink. A large one.

When she had left the house, Hilary had no idea where she was going. She simply turned up her raincoat collar and started walking. The streets were deserted. And odd car or bus passed throwing up a shower of water as it went by. Hilary could see the faces of the passengers peering out at her, wondering why anyone would want to be out on a night like this. She walked on, up the hill to the shops and then left by the big old church and down towards the park.

Her hair was soaking wet under the thin headscarf and her feet were almost afloat in her shoes. Half an hour later she found herself in Waverly Gardens. She realized with a start that she must have walked round in an enormous circle. Waverly Gardens was just round the corner from where she and Roger lived.

Hilary couldn't remember ever having walked down the road before and yet she felt as if somehow she had some link with it. She looked at the houses. They were large, Victorian houses, many of them obviously split and let as flats or bedsits.

She stopped outside number 16 and looked up to see a woman signalling to her from an upstairs window. Hilary peered through the rain and darkness in an effort to make out who it was. The woman looked familiar. Surely it was the same lady she'd spoken to in the coffee shop.

The window opened and Hilary heard her name being called.

'Mrs Wright, Mrs Wright! I'm coming down.'

Hilary waited by the front gate and a minute later saw Carol Coren open the front door and step out into the porch.

'I'm sorry if I startled you,' Carol said. 'But I saw you going by, all wet . . . and I wondered if you'd like to come in for a cup of something. You know, to warm you up.'

Hilary was about to say, no. That she lived just round the corner and ought to be getting back, but instead heard herself saying, yes. She followed Carol up the narrow stairs to a large room on the first floor.

'I'll put the kettle on,' Carol said and popped into a small kitchenette that led off the main room. 'Take your coat and shoes off,' she shouted over her shoulder, 'I'll get a towel.'

Hilary started to say it was all right, but stopped herself. The woman, Carol, seemed to get pleasure from doing things for other people, so why spoil it for her. And she certainly could do with drying off. Hilary looked at her watch. It was 10 o'clock. She mustn't stay too long.

Carol came back with a towel and insisted on drying Hilary's feet for her. Then she lit the small gas fire despite the sultriness of the evening and draped Hilary's raincoat over a chair in front of it.

'The loo's just across the hall, if you want it,' Carol said, handing Hilary a mugful of steaming hot coffee.

'Thank you,' Hilary said and sipped at the coffee. Now she was here, she wasn't sure why she'd agreed to come in and have a drink. She couldn't think what to talk about. But she needn't have worried. Carol rattled on about this and that, and about the accident. And finally, about the coincidence of their being born in the same village.

Hilary was intrigued and suddenly found herself telling Carol Coren all about herself and about the change in her relationship with Roger since the accident.

At 11 o'clock Roger decided to go to bed. There was still no sign of Hilary. Outside there was a distant rumble of thunder and the odd flash of lightning that flickered through the bedroom curtains. The house seemed particularly quiet. Normally you could hear the floorboards creak or the water gurgling through the pipes, but tonight everything was still and hushed. Only the noise of the approaching storm broke the heavy, threatening silence. Roger pulled a sheet over him and drifted, gratefully, into an uneasy sleep.

He woke again abruptly three quarters of an hour later. The storm had broken overhead. Great flashes of lightning flashed across the sky lighting up the landscape like some midnight sun. Wave after wave of thunder crashed and rolled around the heavens.

Beside him Hilary, naked on top of the bed, writhed and moaned in her sleep as if possessed by a thousand devils. Roger looked at his watch. It was nearly midnight. Outside the wind howled round the chimney pots and the bedroom curtains billowed out into the room like the sails on a boat.

A bolt of thunder crashed above their heads. Hilary woke with a start and looked round wildly, as if unsure of where she was. Roger put his arm out towards her. 'It's all right. There's a storm,' he said gently. She turned towards him and put her arms round him. Her body felt taut and excited. There was a wild look in her eyes. Slowly at first, and then with an increasing urgency Hilary started to rub her body against his.

Roger felt the excitement start to rise in him. Hilary started moaning, he couldn't understand what it was she was saying, but he knew that she was urging, begging him to make love to her.

'Are you sure it's all right?' Roger asked. 'So soon after the baby?'

She nodded her head violently and pulled him closer towards her. Roger's hands reached down and started to caress her. She was shaking all over.

'Now! Roger now!' she cried.

Roger started to make love to her, but she turned away from him. He watched her as she crouched on all fours, her jet black hair resting on the pillows at the head of the bed. Her skin was shining with moisture, her body tense with expectation. Roger had never seen Hilary like this, she was like an animal on heat.

'Please! Roger please!' she moaned.

Roger knelt up behind her and thrust himself deep inside her. Hilary gasped under the force of his attack and then cried out in pleasure as he started to move in and out of her.

The electricity in the air seemed to find an outlet in their love-making. Roger had never known anything like it. Their bodies were on fire. They were like two rutting animals, oblivious of anything and everything other than their lust. Roger felt Hilary start to shudder under him.

She raised her head up from the pillows and started to toss it from side to side. Her long black hair whipping at his body and her urgent, obscene cries drove Roger to a fury of excitement. He felt all control slipping away from him. And then there was nothing. Everything was lost in the great molten river that seemed to join their two bodies.

It seemed to be at that moment, that the storm reached its height. The bedroom was filled with a great, white light and thunder crashed and rolled across the sky. Some force seemed to draw Roger's eyes towards the small open window above the bed.

The wind had forced the curtains apart and Roger found himself staring into a huge pair of brilliant green eyes. They were the eyes of the most perfect cat he had ever seen. It was more than just a cat. It was a work of art. Roger couldn't stop looking at the face. It was beautiful. Almost human, and yet perfect, pure animal at the same time.

The cat looked at him for a long minute and in that time Roger knew that the cat somehow spelt danger for him. He tried to say something, to tell Hilary, but no words would come. And then the cat was gone, as suddenly and as completely as it had appeared. For a moment Roger wondered if it was some apparition brought about by the storm. But the thought only lasted a minute. Roger knew that whatever the explanation, the cat was real enough. And so was the danger he felt so close to him.

He looked across at Hilary, she lay in a deep, almost trance-like sleep, a half-smile on her face. Roger got up from the bed, put on his dressing gown and went into his study. The storm had passed. The wind had dropped and stars were back in the sky. The heaviness of the previous day had gone, too. And yet he still felt the same strangeness in the air, the same uncertainty. Roger sat at his desk for a long while before going back to bed.

* * *

The morning after the storm was clear and bright and sunny. It was almost as if the storm and the events preceeding it had never happened. Almost, but not quite. Certainly for some people Thursday the eleventh was a day they would never forget. For others it was something they read about in their morning papers or heard about on the radio or on television.

Ian Wert woke slowly from his long sedated sleep. He lay in bed, smoking a cigarette, waiting for his mother to bring him a cup of tea. His chief memory of the previous day was Pat and the seeing to he'd given her in the afternoon. That and the fact that he'd missed his date with her in the evening and the chance to get it away again. Never mind, he promised himself, there would be other times. Maybe he'd ring her at dinner time and explain.

Ian stubbed out the cigarette on a saucer by his bed. He put his hand up to his face and traced the pattern of scars with his fingers. They were dry. There was no blood. And there was no pain. Everything was back to normal. He reached out and took out another cigarette just as his mother walked in with the tea.

Hilary was up early the morning after the storm. She had slept well after making love with Roger and she felt ready to pick up the threads of her life again. The tension she'd felt recently had gone. She wanted to do something. She needed an interest in life, other than the house and looking after Roger. If there was to be no baby for the moment, then she would plan her life accordingly.

Hilary realized that whenever she thought about the baby, or about there not being a baby, she added the words 'for the moment', to herself. She didn't know why. She had heard what Dr Willis had said about not being able to have children. He had explained it all very clearly. And at the time she had accepted it. But somehow, since she'd been home, she'd become less and less convinced.

She had nothing to go on, no medical opinion, just a feeling that there would be a baby, sometime in the future. It was not something she talked to Roger about. Or to anyone else, for that matter, with the exception of Carol Coren. But then Hilary had found herself telling Carol a lot of things that she'd never told anyone before.

Roger came down to breakfast full of hope. It had been a strange night. And the feeling of unease was still with him. But he did hope that Hilary wanting to make love, even in so wild a fashion, was a sign that things were on the mend between them. Perhaps, at the very least, it meant that the old closeness they had shared was not dead.

'Morning,' he said, kissing her on the cheek.

'Hello.'

'Did you sleep well?' Roger asked.

'Mmm,' Hilary said, stretching. 'Did you?'

'Some of the time,' Roger answered in an attempt to bring up the subject of their love-making. He wanted to hear Hilary acknowledge that it had been good. Fantastic. And to say how much she loved him.

'I think I'm going to take a course,' Hilary said.

'What kind of course, darling?'

'Oh, I don't know, I thought I'd go down to the Adult Education Centre and see what there was. I'm bored here, Roger. And now there's not going to be a baby I need more to do.'

Roger thought for a moment.

'Why don't you re-decorate the nursery?' he suggested. 'I'll help. We could turn it into a sort of den for you. You know, you could keep all your sewing things in there and . . .'

Roger stopped in mid-sentence. Hilary was shaking her head violently.

'Hilary, it's got to be faced,' Roger said gently. 'You just said so yourself. There's no point in . . .'

For the second time Roger was halted half-way through his sentence as Hilary rushed out of the kitchen, along the hall and into the downstairs lavatory.

Roger followed her.

'Hilary! Are you all right?'

Hilary didn't answer, but Roger heard her retching into the lavatory bowl. He went back to the kitchen and poured himself another cup of tea. Ten minutes later Hilary returned looking white-faced.

'Feel better?'

Hilary nodded.

'Want another cup of tea.'

'Yes, please.' She sat down and rested her elbows on the kitchen table.

'I wonder what brought that on,' Roger said.

'Well, if I didn't know better, I'd say I was pregnant,' she answered.

'Do you mean it?'

'Yes. It was just like the morning sickness I had a few months ago.'

'It's a bit quick,' Roger said, referring once again to the previous night.

Hilary didn't say anything, she just sipped at her tea and looked thoughtful. She was remembering the other strange thoughts and feelings she'd had yesterday.

And the previous night, that Roger seemed so keen to talk about. She remembered it, all of it, clearly, although she was not ready to admit it to Roger. She had seen the cat too. And the way it had looked at Roger. It had made her feel sorry for him, but she wasn't sure why.

Hilary had felt drawn to the cat. It was almost as if it were part of her, or she was part of it. Even after it had vanished so suddenly, Hilary could still feel and sense its presence. If anything it seemed nearer. At times she could almost hear it talking to her. It reminded her of the voice she had heard at the accident and in the hospital. The voice she had to answer.

'I think you ought to see the doctor,' Roger said in a concerned voice.

'I'll make an appointment.'

'Do you want me to come?'

'No.' And then because she had sounded sharper than she'd meant to, she added, 'No, thank you, darling, I'd rather do it on my own.'

After Roger had gone, not very happily, to work, Hilary wondered why she'd said no to his offer. In the past they had always done everything like that together. She knew Roger was hurt and puzzled, but she couldn't help it. She wanted to be on her own. Independent. Free to go off if and when she wanted to. And anyway what had it got to do with Roger? How she felt and what happened to her body was her concern. Roger was too much sometimes, he fussed, and that got on her nerves.

Helen Champion had been a nurse for five years. And for the last three of those five years she'd been at St Michael's Hospital. During her time there the attractive twenty-four year-old blonde had made a lot of friends. Helen had always been an outgoing girl and had found in nursing a natural outlet for her sunny disposition and her need to live life to the full.

Patients and staff responded to her openness and from the moment she'd joined St Michael's she had been overwhelmed with invitations to parties, dinners, dances and the like. She had joined the Hospital Tennis Club, and she had swum for them in the London Hospitals Cup. But Helen was a sensible girl too. And she had always made time to continue her studies and to take the exams needed to get on in her profession. She had taken her SRN two years ago and then had applied to become a theatre nurse. A year ago her application had been granted.

The hours were sometimes long, and the work hard, physically and emotionally, but Helen enjoyed it. A year ago she had met Charles Goodman, a young intern, and despite her previous determination not to get serious with anyone, had fallen like a ton of bricks for the tall, rather studious young doctor.

Helen had often wondered how it had happened. Charles was not exactly her type. And they certainly didn't share that many interests in common. But it worked for both of them. And the last year had been the happiest of Helen's life.

She had written to her parents about Charles and talked endlessly about him on her weekend visits back to the Lake District. But so far they had not met him. Somehow their time off had never really coincided, and at first Helen had wanted to keep Charles to herself. At least until she was really sure about how she felt.

But now she was certain. And so was Charles and this weekend they were going up to Appleby so that he could meet her mum and dad and tell them they were going to get engaged. Helen was looking forward to walking in the hills and showing Charles the lakes and little villages around her home. She knew too that her mum and dad would like Charles and that he would get on with them.

Helen looked at her watch. It was 4 o'clock and time for her to go off duty for four whole days! Charles was going to pick her up at the flat at 6 o'clock. That meant she'd have plenty of time to wash her hair and have a bath before she started on the packing.

She decided to walk home in her uniform. It wasn't far and it would save changing twice. She gathered up her hand-bag and some shopping she'd done on the way in, took one last look round the staff room and started off for home.

As she walked along the wide, echoing corridors Helen couldn't help wondering what people would say on Tuesday when she and Charles came back and announced their engagement. Several of her friends knew that they were close, but Helen hadn't told anyone about their plans to get married.

She said goodnight to George, the hospital porter, and turned left into Hallow Street. The fresh air felt good. It had been a busy day and the journey home to Appleby was going to take a good six hours.

Helen started to make a mental note of things she needed to pack. The walk from the hospital to home was automatic after three years. Halfway down Heston Avenue she turned off into Canberry Gardens. Nearly all the leaves were off the trees now, but she still liked the little park. It was like a little bit of the countryside in the middle of London. And the big rhododendron bushes were still green.

The place was deserted today. Helen shivered and pulled the collar of her coat up round her neck. The afternoons and evenings were beginning to draw in. She went past the bandstand and then down the narrow, almost overgrown path that led to the tennis courts. It was a short-cut she and Charles had discovered, that saved them three or four valuable minutes when they came together in the mornings.

Helen was almost at the end of the pathway when she heard a noise. A funny sort of half-cry from the bushes on her left. She stopped and listened, but the sound had stopped. Helen shrugged her shoulders and started on her way. But she had only taken a step when she heard the sound again.

And this time there was movement amongst the branches of the bushes that made the shiny green leaves rustle.

Helen turned and peered through the foliage. She couldn't see anything.

And then she heard the sound again. A voice, surely it

was a voice. Thin and scratchy almost like a cat meowing. But Helen was sure it had said, 'Help me'.

She pushed her way into the undergrowth and there in front of her was the sweetest little grey and white kitten she had ever seen. It looked as if it was caught between two branches that had grown around one another.

Helen smiled and laughed at herself, voices indeed! For a moment, back on the path, she'd felt quite frightened. She reached up towards the kitten. 'Come here, you little monkey,' she said. 'You gave me quite a shock. Never mind, we'll soon have you down.'

The kitten looked at her and started to open its tiny mouth. But it didn't meow. It laughed. A hideous laugh! And as it laughed its small delicate face grew larger, and a look of evil replaced the innocence that had been there a minute before.

Helen screamed in horror and stepped back, desperate to get away from the thing. A branch cut across her face and then just as suddenly as the thing had appeared, it vanished.

Helen gave a sigh of relief and started to make her way back to the path. It was then she realized that she was not alone.

Chapter Seven

Helen couldn't see who it was behind her. But she could feel breath on the back of her neck and the weight of another body pressing against hers.

She tried to turn round so that she could see who it was. Or what it was. No, she was being silly. The cat had frightened her. She must be sensible. 'Excuse me, please,' she said politely, but firmly, and started to turn again so that she could get back on to the path.

There was no answer. Helen felt her legs start to tremble. 'A cat got caught . . . in the tree,' she said, for no reason. 'And then it turned . . . who are you?' Helen whispered and felt tears start to run down her cheek.

There was still no answer. But Helen could feel whoever it was starting to press closer to her. She felt rather than saw an arm start to encircle her waist. It felt strong.

Helen kicked back with all her strength. She felt her foot connect with something but there was no cry of pain. She started to run forward and for a moment thought she had got away.

But then there was the sound of someone behind her and she knew that whoever it was had only to reach out and get her.

She ran faster, tearing her face and her uniform on the branches of the rhododendron bushes. Her tights were in holes, her legs and hands bleeding. Tears and blood ran down her cheeks as she sobbed and choked her way forward.

Helen didn't see the rock, half buried in the ground, until it was too late. Suddenly she felt herself falling forward. And as she fell she knew that it was the end of her.

Whoever it was meant to kill her, and she knew that she no longer had the strength to stop them. She lay with her face pressed against the damp earth and the rotting leaves, trembling from head to foot with fear.

For a minute everything was quiet. And then she heard the laugh. The same awful, sick laugh the thing had screamed out earlier.

Helen forced herself to roll over on to her back so that she could see what kind of madman was intent on killing her. Maybe she could plead with him. She'd do anything, anything, if he'd just let her go.

But what Helen saw when she looked up froze the wor ds she'd prepared on her breath. She knew finally there was no hope. No words that would move nor any bargain, however degrading, that could be struck.

In the seconds that Helen Champion had left to live she thought about Charles and her parents. And the weekend that was to have been the happiest of her life.

And then she felt the pain as her throat was ripped across from ear to ear. And the wetness as her bowels opened at the sheer terror of what was happening and what was still to happen.

It was an old lady who found her body. Or what was left of it. The entrails had been laid out, mostly hidden by the bushes. But not quite.

And there was another curious fact about the death. There was one organ missing.

The first news of the murder came on the 9 o'clock news. There was no name given, and very few details. But in an interview with a BBC reporter, Chief Superintendent Wilson did confirm that the killing was a particularly nasty one.

He urged anyone who had been in or around the Canberry Gardens area between 3 o'clock and 6 o'clock to get in touch with the police if they had seen or heard anything that might help the investigation.

That was the extent of any public statement the police were making, but privately not a few officers drafted on to the case were already beginning to talk about another 'Ripper' case.

One reason was the way in which the entrails had been laid out and the fact that one organ was missing. It was as if the murderer wanted his grisly work to be noticed, to be commented on. As if he wanted to make sure that it was not to be confused with any ordinary murder. There was a ritual that gave warning to those who regularly dealt with murder that there might be more to come.

Dr Willis had been informed of Helen Champion's murder by phone. He was deeply shocked. Being a senior medical man at St Michael's he had been given the full details of the crime. And those had shocked him even more than the initial news of Helen's death.

After the phone call he had sat in the lounge of his small house in Barnes staring out of the window into the darkness for a long time. He was trying to put out of his mind the thought that had almost immediately flown there on hearing the news.

It was preposterous. Unbelievable. And yet the world was full of unbelievable things that were nevertheless accepted as fact. There were also many, many things that science, even in its advanced state, could not explain.

But this? Well, this was something out of some horror film. Perhaps, Dr Willis thought, he ought to see one of his colleagues. Talk it out with someone. But how could you explain you were being watched by a cat, day and night? And that somehow you knew the cat had something to do with the thing that he had delivered to Mrs Wright after the accident?

And now there was Helen Champion's murder and all he could think about were the marks on the cupboard door. Marks that had been made by someone, no, something, that was enormously strong and that had claws that were incredibly sharp. Strong enough and sharp enough to tear the body of a healthy young girl apart.

Dr Willis poured himself a drink – a very strong drink – and went back and sat in his chair. He knew there was no chance of explaining the suspicion that lurked in his mind, to anyone.

He was alone with his ghastly thoughts. And with the premonition of his own death that was getting stronger with each night's uneasy sleep.

Roger had unburdened himself to Steve over a beer and a sandwich at lunch. He had told him everything about the night before and the events of the following morning.

Steve had listened sympathetically but had not been able to offer anything very tangible in the way of help, other than a renewed invitation to bring Hilary to dinner so they could all try and 'Cheer her up a bit'. He had suggested Monday night. And Roger had promised to speak to Hilary that evening.

To his surprise Hilary had said yes, and he had rung Steve and accepted right away, before she could change her mind. Roger had asked Hilary how she felt the minute he'd got home, but in view of her reaction earlier in the day he had deliberately not asked if she had been to see the doctor. Hilary had not mentioned it either. And for the last half an hour Roger had been wondering whether to bring the subject up. Hilary seemed all right, still not her old affectionate self, but not quite as remote as she had been recently.

The television was on and they were both sitting on the little two-seater settee with a mug of coffee each. A government spokesman had just finished dealing with the latest unemployment figures. The scene changed and the murder of an unnamed nurse was announced. The two of them listened in silence. No mention was made of St Michael's Hospital, but the report gave Roger a funny feeling. It also prompted him to ask Hilary about the doctor.

'I haven't been yet,' she said with a coldness that clearly indicated the subject was closed.

But Roger was not prepared to be put off. He was worried about Hilary. True, she looked well enough. In fact, very well considering what she'd been through, but looks and physical health were only half of it. And over the last two days, Roger had begun to wonder whether Hilary wasn't on the verge of a mental breakdown.

She had never been able to take a lot of pressure. She had always needed his reassurance, his help to sort things out in her own mind, before she could deal with them.

Roger had put it down to the sheltered early life she'd led. He knew that when she had left the convent she knew very little about the outside world and how it functioned.

Even when he'd met her, after she'd been working in London for a year or so, Hilary had been very uncertain. Then there was another coldness about her, a purity that had made her different from the other girls he knew.

Roger remembered that on their first date he had hardly dared kiss her for fear of shocking her. But he needn't have worried. Hilary had liked kissing. And the two of them were soon head over heels in love with each other.

But everything had changed since the accident. And the change was worrying Roger. He was worried about Hilary but also about the effect the change was having on his work.

He was finding it hard to concentrate. And he knew his writing was not as sharp as it usually was.

He'd not told Hilary, but he'd spent the latter part of the afternoon walking round town trying to sort out his thoughts. And trying to think of something to do that would get the two of them back together again.

He moved a little closer and put an arm round Hilary's shoulder.

'Darling, I really do think you ought to do something about it.'

Hilary didn't say anything. Roger could feel the stiffness in her. And he knew that she did not want his arm around her. He tried again.

'Hilary, what's the matter?'

She shrugged her shoulders. 'Nothing.'

'But there is, can't you see that? This morning you were sick and you said it was like being pregnant. And there was last night . . . you're not the same two days running. I know it's been a shock for you but we've got to do something about it. We can't go on like this.'

'You can't, you mean. There's nothing wrong with me.' She started to get up.

'Don't go,' Roger said and pulled at her arm with his hand. 'We've got to talk.'

Hilary turned on him her eyes blazing.

'I don't want to talk,' she screamed and struck at his hand in an attempt to loosen his hold. Roger felt her nails rake across the back of his hand and cried out in pain. Three thin rivers of blood started to work their way down between his knuckles and on to his fingers.

'Just keep away from me!' Hilary said and stalked out of the room. Five minutes later he heard the front door slam.

Helen Champion's death meant little to Ian Wert. True it was blazoned all over the front page of his daily newspaper, but then Ian was in the habit of reading the back page of the newspaper first and then working his way forward, as it were, through the funnies and the centre spread to page three.

It was only when his mother pointed out the three inch high headline 'New Ripper Attack' that he even acknowledged the paper in question had a front page.

When he had read the story, the name of Helen Champion still meant nothing to him. Nor for that matter did the large rather attractive photograph. But the name of St Michael's Hospital made him stop and think for a minute. He wondered if she was one of the nurses who'd looked after him. There were a couple of really tasty ones there all right. Not that it had done him much good.

Ian put the paper down and lit another cigarette. He'd swore he was going to get even but as yet he'd done nothing about it. He wondered what they were up to. Perhaps he'd go and find out. He had their address on a piece of paper somewhere. Somehow it didn't seem quite so important as it had. The insurance company had paid up good for once and he was going out to buy a new motor. The scars on his face didn't seem to put any of the birds off and the peculiar markings gave him a look of toughness that he rather enjoyed. Still he'd said he'd get even and get even he would.

He looked at the front of the paper and suddenly he had it. It would be so simple. A telephone call or a letter and bingo. Mr Roger bleeding Wright would be right in it, up to his unmarked little neck. He'd read about that kind of thing in books.

Of course, he realized that it wouldn't last for long, the law would soon find out who had killed Helen Champion. Or, at least, that Wright hadn't, but in the meantime, the trouble it might cause would serve the silly bugger right.

When she'd left the house the previous night, Hilary had no idea where she was going. But by the time she'd reached the front gate she had decided to go and see Carol Coren. Carol had been so sympathetic before and she'd said to drop in whenever Hilary felt like it.

The two of them had talked for a long time as Hilary had explained how she felt. Hilary couldn't remember now whether she or Carol had thought of the idea. They'd been talking about losing the baby and the idea of getting a cat as company for Hilary was suddenly born.

Hilary had not mentioned the idea to Roger. She knew he wasn't very keen on pets. Steve and Sue always had to keep Buster out of the way whenever she and Roger went over there to dinner. Somehow, she'd have to introduce the thought slowly and win Roger round.

Maybe Sue would help her. Perhaps she'd get her alone when they went over on Monday night. In the meantime, Hilary decided, it would do no harm to find out a little more about the subject. There was a pet shop in that little parade past the park: she'd go and talk to them. And there was always the library, there were bound to be books on cats there. If she left it till the afternoon perhaps Carol would like to go with her.

It was strange, Hilary thought, how she kept thinking of Carol when she wanted company and was upset with Roger. But then the whole situation was strange. Fancy Carol being born in the same village. And then being so close on the night of the accident. It was almost as if it had been planned. But that was silly.

Hilary wondered whether Carol's parents had known hers. She hadn't asked last evening, maybe she would tonight. Aunt Joan had never been very keen to talk to her about her parents, particularly her mother. When she was young, it had made Hilary wonder whether there had been something wrong, something bad, that had to be kept secret.

As it turned out the whole evening was spent talking about the cat. And making plans for the visit to the library and the pet shop the next day.

The trip to the library went well enough. Carol was waiting for Hilary when she got there and the two of them spent the next half an hour looking through the many books on pets of every description.

The trip to the pet shop did not go quite so smoothly. It

was a large pet shop with many kinds of pets in stock. They were housed in cages stacked high around the walls of the shop.

It was 4.30 and many of the animals were asleep when Hilary and Carol went into the shop. And that was what was so strange, because within 2 or 3 minutes of Hilary walking through the door, they were all wide awake. And more, they were making a noise that might have woken the dead.

For Carol it was an immediate and amazing confirmation of the story that surrounded Hilary's birth.

For Hilary it came as a shock. She didn't know what was happening but she did know that it was something to do with her presence that had caused the animals to react in such a way.

They had quickly chosen a book on cat care, to go with the two on the history of the cat they'd got from the library, and made their escape.

Carol suggested they have a cup of tea back at her place. And Hilary agreed. When they were both settled in easy chairs, Carol told Hilary the story about her birth that had gone round the village.

Hilary was intrigued. Almost pleased with the strangeness of the story. In a strange way it seemed to make her more determined than ever to have a cat.

Before Roger came home Hilary hid the books in the dining room. She also washed her hair and put on a dress that she knew Roger liked. The evening passed well enough and not for the first time Roger went to bed hoping that perhaps Hilary had turned the corner and was on the way back to being her old sweet self.

On Saturday morning, the police came and interviewed Roger for the first time. They explained they had received an anonymous letter linking him with the murder of Helen Champion. The sergeant was sympathetic, but insistent on getting detailed answers to his enquiries. Where had

Roger been on the afternoon in question? At work? Could he prove it?

'Yes, of course!' Roger had replied indignantly. And completely forgot that Thursday was the afternoon he'd taken off.

'That's a nasty scratch you've got on your hand, sir,' the sergeant pointed out. 'How did you get it?'

Roger looked across at Hilary and saw her blush. He didn't want to embarrass her, but he didn't know what to say.

'I, er . . .'

'I did it,' Hilary said.

'We were playing about,' Roger added and felt himself blush. The explanation didn't sound very convincing.

'It's quite a deep scratch, isn't it, sir?'

'Yes,' Roger agreed. 'Er, things got a bit out of hand.'

Eventually, Sergeant Childs had left. But had warned Roger that he might be needed again. The rest of the weekend went very slowly.

On Monday the police were round at Roger's office. After asking some questions round the agency, Sergeant Childs asked Roger to go with them to the police station. It was as he got into the police car that Roger remembered that Thursday afternoon was the afternoon he'd taken off. His heart sank. He tried desperately to remember where he'd gone, and if he'd seen anyone.

At the station Sergeant Childs was joined by Inspector Mullery and this time the tone wasn't so sympathetic. Why had he lied about being in the office all Thursday afternoon? Where had he been? What had he been doing? Had he seen anyone who could corroborate his story?

And so the questions went on. For Roger it was a nightmare as he desperately tried to convince the police that his answers were honest, that he had nothing to do with any murder. Of course, the police knew that both Hilary and Roger had been taken to St Michael's after the accident. And that was where the question of motive came in. Helen Champion had been on duty the night of the accident. She had been one of the theatre sisters who'd attended Hilary's operation. Was he sure he didn't feel resentment against her? Against the hospital perhaps, for what had happened to the baby?

No! No! No! Roger shouted the answers in despair as the two policemen asked more and more questions of him. And still he hadn't been allowed to make a phone call to his solicitor. No-one knew where he was, except Steve, who'd only been able to look on in vain as Roger had explained where the police were taking him.

After an hour the two policemen went off for a cup of tea. Roger was left sitting at the bare wooden table with a solitary, uniformed constable to stand guard over him.

He tried desperately to retrace his movements on the previous Thursday. Where had he been? Who had he seen, who could prove he was miles away from St Michael's? Most of the time he'd wandered around in a total daze trying to decide what to do about Hilary, getting angrier and angrier in the process.

Angry! That was it! Maybe the man in the Shepherds Arms would remember him. Roger had felt like a drink, seen the pub door was open and walked in and ordered a large whisky. But it was only 5.15 and the barman or publican, Roger didn't know which, had told him they weren't open.

The bad mood he was in already, with Hilary, himself and life in general, had spilt over on to the man behind the bar. Roger had told him what he could do with his large whisky, his beer pumps and his pub.

The man told Roger to come back the next morning when he wasn't so busy and repeat what he just said. If he dared! After another bad-tempered exchange, Roger had left to continue his lonely walk, but not before he'd made a note of the pub name.

Roger asked the police constable to get Sergeant Childs back to the interview room. Twenty minutes later they were on their way to the Shepherds Arms.

The two police officers went into the pub on their own. Roger waited, hardly daring to hope. Sergeant Childs appeared in the saloon bar doorway and beckoned to the constable to bring Roger into the pub.

Before letting them in, Childs warned Roger not to say anything until he was told to speak. Roger nodded. His throat went dry. Childs opened the door and the three of them stepped into the bar.

Roger recognized the man immediately and he was sure the man recognized him. But he didn't say anything. Not for a long minute. It was the longest minute of Roger's life. And then, 'That's him. Bloody madman. I said to Mary afterwards, the way he was going on he'd end up in trouble.'

Roger started to say something, but Inspector Mullery cut him short.

'And you're quite sure about the day and the time?' he asked the barman.

The barman nodded. 'Quite sure. It's like I said, Inspector, I remember quite clearly because . . .'

The Inspector didn't let him finish. 'Yes, I don't think we need to go into all of it again. We may need you to sign a statement confirming everything you've told us, would you be willing to do that?'

'Yes.'

'And be prepared to swear to it in court?'

'Yes. I told you. I'm quite sure.'

'Take him outside,' Mullery said, nodding at Roger.

'Bloody madman!' The barman called after him, but Roger was too relieved to take any notice.

If Roger had thought he was finished with police, he was wrong. True the tone of voice was nicer, more polite, but still there were questions to be answered. Did he have any enemies? Who had known about the accident? Had he upset any of the hospital staff? But at least he got to make the phone calls he wanted. One to Hilary and the other to Steve.

Steve promised to make his excuses at the agency and tell the Creative Director that everything was all right.

'Listen, Rog, do you want to call this evening off?' Steve asked. 'You know Susie and I will understand. It must have been a nightmare for you.'

'No, Steve. I've spoken to Hilary and she suggested the same thing, but quite honestly I could do with some company. I'm going home to have a bath and then we'll be over about seven-thirty.'

'All right, we'll be waiting with a large something or other,' Steve promised and hung up.

What Roger had told Steve about his conversation with Hilary was factually correct. Hilary had suggested they put off their visit to the Palmers, but her tone of voice had made it very clear that she didn't want to. Roger couldn't help wondering if her reason for wanting to keep the date was the same as his. An unwillingness to spend another evening in together, with all the dramas that seemed to bring these days. Tonight, of all nights, Roger wanted a friendly face about him.

Roger Wright wasn't the only one having a bad day. Dr Willis hadn't been questioned by the police, but the murder and its effect on the hospital staff was causing him severe problems. And the problems were not made any easier by his tiredness and the general state of his nerves.

The Ripper Story run by certain newspapers had led to a demand from some of the younger nurses that a patrol be organized, at least in the area between the hospital and the nurses' home. It was quite impossible, of course, but convincing the deputation had taken time. In the end the hospital had asked the police to put an extra man or two on that beat. And the nurses had been advised to go to and from the hospital in pairs, whenever possible.

It had all taken time. A lot of time. As had the other business of the hospital. But it was not those problems, or the time taken to deal with them, that worried Dr Willis. He was used to that. No, it was his personal reaction to those problems. It was the anger, the immeasurable anger that threatened to explode at any minute that really worried him. It was anger caused by fear. And Dr Willis could feel that fear spreading inside of him like an evil cancer.

He had begun taking valium regularly, but it was not enough to combat the feeling of near panic he felt at the sight of the cat that seemed to follow him everywhere. He had gone on to stronger drugs, although it was against every principle he believed in, but the slight relief had lasted only a day or two.

Since the death of Helen Champion, the cat seemed more self-assured. At first when Dr Willis looked at the jet black face there was almost a smile in the cold green eyes that seemed to say, 'I told you so'.

Recently Dr Willis had taken to closing the curtains in whatever room he was in. It didn't matter whether it was night or day, but he still couldn't get away from the thing. A gust of wind would cause the curtains to open or the blind to snap up and there it was, just sitting looking at him.

Dr Willis took out a syringe and filled it with morphine. He put a tourniquet on his left arm and pushed the needle firmly into the bulging vein.

Chapter Eight

The evening had gone better than Roger had expected. Hilary, despite her slight coldness on the phone, had been sympathetic when he'd got home. She had even come and talked to him as he bathed and got ready to go out, just like she used to in the old days, before the accident.

They had decided not to take the car, but to go by underground and come back by mini-cab. That way neither of them had to worry about what they drank, or how late they stayed.

Steve had been as good as his word: there was a bottle of champagne waiting for them when they arrived and the four of them were soon chattering away about Roger's dreadful ordeal.

It was Hilary who, when the first bottle of champagne had run dry, suggested that Steve and Roger go to the pub and get another.

When they got back Hilary had been playing with Buster, the Palmers' cat. The sight had stopped Roger in his tracks. Memories of the storm and the black cat that had seemed to stare at him so intently, came flooding back. For a moment Roger had felt afraid.

The light-hearted mood of relief brought on by the champagne and the Palmers' friendship vanished. Hilary had noticed immediately, so too had Steve and Sue. They had put the cat outside and opened the second bottle of champagne, but it had taken half an hour before they were all at ease again.

The rest of the evening had been a success. Sue was a good cook and the dinner was delicious. There was more wine and brandy and coffee to finish up with.

There was just one odd moment. Hilary had left the room saying she was going to powder her nose. At the time, Roger had thought nothing of it. But after she had been gone a good ten minutes he had excused himself saying he had better go and see if she was all right. He had found her in the kitchen with the cat.

There was nothing strange in that. It was just that the minute before he entered the room, Roger could have sworn that he'd heard her talking to somebody. And somebody was answering her.

He couldn't hear what was being said. And that was the strangest part of all. Roger was quite sure that the conversation was being held in some strange language that he'd never heard before in his life.

Roger and Hilary had left the Palmers' house at one o'clock in the morning. All four friends agreed that it had been a really good evening and that they must do it again, soon. It had been good, Sue was the first to agree, but before she went to sleep she couldn't help making a point to Steve that had been nagging at her all evening.

'What did you think of Hilary this evening?'

'She seemed fine. Just like her old self, why?'

'Well that's exactly the point. I mean, from what Roger had told you I expected her to be a bit strange.'

Steve yawned. 'Yes, I see what you mean.'

'I thought it was Roger who was a bit funny, if you really want to know,' Sue said.

'He's had a hard time recently. The police thing must have been the end coming after the accident and everything else.'

'Mmm. But did you see him when he saw Hilary playing with Buster. I thought he was going to freak out completely. And he was funny for half an hour after that. I mean, I know he doesn't like cats but he looked scared stiff. As if he'd seen a ghost. I don't think Hilary's going to win that one.'

Steve opened his eyes.

'Win what one?'

'Oh, I forgot! You were at the pub. Well, Hilary wants a cat and she was asking me about Buster and how we got him. But somehow after seeing Roger's face when you came back from the pub I don't think anything I told her will make much difference, because she's not going to get to first base.'

Steve turned over.

'She'll probably find a way,' he said over his shoulder. 'You women usually do.'

Jean Merrow was not what you'd call pretty. Or, for that matter, even attractive, but she had a very good figure, long shapely legs and long auburn hair that came nearly down to her waist. She also liked men. She liked them a lot. And maybe for that reason they seemed to like her.

She was good fun, Jean Merrow. That's what they said. You could have a good time with her and there were no questions asked about tomorrow or, when am I going to see you again? In fact, it was the opposite.

It was Jean who decided if she wanted to see you again. And if she did, when she wanted to see you. And Jean Merrow's talents at love-making were such that there weren't many men who refused a return engagement.

For a few people, both men and women, Jean Merrow was little more than a common whore. Their opinion as to what should be done with her varied, but those of them at St Michael's all thought that she was a disgrace to the nursing profession and to the hospital service and that she should be asked to leave both.

They were wrong, because Jean was a very good nurse. And even if they'd been right, it would have been very difficult for anyone at St Michael's to have got rid of her.

Jean Merrow had only been at the hospital for 3 years, but in that time her eye and more particularly her shapely body had fallen on many of the staff there, right up to and including members of the hospital board.

Not that she limited herself to members of the medical profession. Jean had worked hard at her choice of job. She had noticed that people liked nurses and she wanted, needed very badly, to be liked. Then too, you came into contact with a lot of people. Jean liked people. She liked talking to them, being with them, doing things for them. Even her mother had said she was a kind girl. And that was praise indeed from Margot Merrow.

And then, of course, last but not least, Jean had noticed that the medical profession attracted a lot of healthy, intelligent, young men who knew how to have a good time.

After that the decision had been easy. Jean had always been a strong-minded girl who inevitably got what she wanted. She had enrolled as a nurse, done her three years training and two years after passing her SRN had become a theatre sister. The work was hard and the pay was poor. But she didn't mind. If Jean had used her sexual talents for money she knew she could have been a rich girl by now. But the thought was totally repugnant to her.

Anyone who thought that she wanted money out of it was wrong. Totally and absolutely wrong. They didn't understand she wasn't like her mother. The exact opposite, in fact.

Her mother had hated sex. Jean remembered her saying that she was nearly sick every time a man entered her. But she never showed it, or if she did men didn't seem to mind. Perhaps it was a kind of turn-on for some of them. What Margot Merrow did like was the power that her sex gave her. And the money she could earn from it.

It had enabled her to educate her family decently, without having to rely on a man. Especially one like Frank, her husband. Not that he'd ever been around much. Or shown any interest in either the family or where they lived after the first two or three years.

When she was young, Jean had often wondered where her mother went to at night, wondered exactly what her mother's job was. Her mother had never brought anyone home to the house and that too had seemed strange to the young, innocent girl, when her mother was so pretty.

And then one day, not long after Jean had discovered the joy of sex herself, her mother had spoken to her and told her everything.

Maybe it was the way her mother had told her, with no feeling of shame, but Jean had felt no sense of shock. She had simply accepted it. And accepted her mother's reasons for telling her. The only sadness she had felt was that her mother got no pleasure from an act that she had to perform so often. After the conversation with her mother, Jean had sworn to herself that she would enjoy the pleasure she got out of making love.

She'd work hard for her money and she'd play hard too, with whoever and whenever she wanted. And that's just what she'd done. She knew that some of the other nurses called her an amateur prostitute and a couple had as good as told her she was a nymphomaniac. But she knew that neither accusation was true. She also knew that many of them were jealous. Jean had been amazed to learn that, like her mother, many of them got no pleasure at all from their love-making, and regarded it as a necessary evil if they were to keep a boyfriend or get a husband. In Jean's eyes their attitude was a good deal more dishonest than hers.

Jean unlocked the door of her flat and walked into the tiny hallway. There were some letters on the mat and she stooped down to pick them up. There were the usual bills and a letter from an ex-boyfriend, who'd moved away, saying he would be in town next week and would love to see her. Jean laughed to herself. She knew what that meant.

She went into the kitchen and made herself a glass of

lemon juice and then started on her beauty routine for the evening. She was seeing Dick Southern, a young and very active gynaecologist, for dinner.

Jean's beauty routine took just over an hour and it was something she did every day of her life. Early on she'd decided that if her body was going to give her so much pleasure, then the least she could do was to look after it. The routine involved a bath or a shower, yoga, some body massage and a session in front of the long mirror in her bedroom when she touched various parts of her body with her hands and with different objects teaching it to respond in new and more pleasurable ways.

This afternoon was no exception. Jean stripped off her clothes and let herself sink into a warm oiled bath. As the water closed over her, she closed her eyes and started to daydream. For this was her private world where no-one else could enter.

Later, dressed only in the softest of towelling robes, she walked through into the bedroom again to begin the second and third parts of her routine.

As she passed the kitchen her attention was caught by a scratching noise at the window. It was the grey and white cat from down the road. It was almost as if it was tapping on the window pane with its paw.

Jean got out a saucer, filled it with milk and then opened the window just enough to let the cat spring over the raised sill, on to the draining-board and down on to the floor where she had placed the saucer.

'Good boy,' Jean said and stroked him under the chin.

The cat purred and brushed itself up against her bare leg. Jean stroked the cat again. She liked the feeling of the soft grey fur against her skin.

She left the cat to drink its milk and went on into the bedroom to concentrate on her yoga exercises. The Fish, the Headstand, The Spinal thrust, the Frog and the exercise she needed to keep her body supple, alive, young.

She was sitting on the floor in front of the long mirror when she heard a movement at the door. Her body stiffened and she caught her breath. Her head swung round, involuntarily, eager yet fearful to see who was there.

The door opened wider. And Jean laughed. It was the cat. It padded over towards her and rubbed itself up against her naked body.

Jean put her hands under the animal's front legs and held it full length against her naked breasts and belly. She could feel herself getting excited. She lay back and stretched out her legs, spreading them slightly apart in the process. She stroked the cat from the top of its head to the end of its long fluffy tail. It settled down, spread out on top of her like some miniature tiger skin rug. Its tail flicked between her legs, creating a little pool of wetness in the process.

And then it happened. Jean could hardly believe it. She closed her eyes and muttered, 'Please don't stop.' The animal was licking her nipples! The roughness of its tongue excited them so that they grew as red and as large as cherries.

The animal moved. Jean held her breath waiting to see what it would do next. She felt a soft claw on the inside of her thigh. It travelled up over her belly. She felt herself tremble.

The paw stroked her again, this time between her legs. This time a little more roughly. But she didn't mind. She knew that any minute now she was going to have an orgasm. She held her breath. A tongue touched her nipple. And bit hard. Jean screamed, but the animal went on biting. She could feel blood running down her body. She tried to get up, but was suddenly aware of more pain.

The dream was turning into a nightmare. She forced herself to open her eyes, only to shut them again at once. She didn't understand. There was more than one cat.

There were five or six of them. And they were eating her alive.

Jean started to call out, but a claw ripped at her tongue tearing it from her throat until it flapped, a shredded and useless mess at her mouth. Pain was everywhere. Red, violent pain that seared through her body but that had a kind of beauty of its own.

Through the pain, Jean felt a paw catch at her pubic hair. It drew a delicate line upwards till it reached the soft swell of her belly.

The paw was withdrawn, only to retrace its journey. This time biting deep into her flesh, tearing skin, membrane and muscle alike. It was the signal for the last savage attack.

The body was found during the early evening. And the news was picked up by both the BBC and ITN in their main evening bulletins. Possibly because they had that little bit longer, ITN made more of the story than the BBC.

A reporter speaking from outside Jean's flat gave details of the gruesome killing. A senior police officer confirmed that there were similarities between the Merrow murder and that of another nurse only a few days before.

There were pictures of St Michael's Hospital and an interview with a young trainee nurse who said she was frightened to go out alone since the murders.

For Dr Willis the second murder, and the hideousness of the wounds inflicted on the body, simply confirmed his worst suspicions. He was sure now without any shadow of doubt that somehow the cat was involved and that sooner or later he would also become its victim.

He had seriously thought about moving. Even leaving the country, but he knew that there could be no escape. Somehow the animal had managed to communicate that to him.

All he could do was wait. And maybe ease the waiting

with some drugs. It didn't seem to matter anymore. Dr Willis knew in his heart of hearts that his time was drawing near.

For Roger, the news of Jean Merrow's death had brought memories of his previous ordeal flooding back to him. And although he knew that he could account for every moment of the day from lunchtime onwards, he still half expected the phone to ring or the doorbell to go.

Hilary was out for a walk. He had offered to go with her, but she had said she preferred to be on her own. Any sign of hope that Roger had seen during the evening with Sue and Steve had completely disappeared. Over the last few days Hilary had seemed more remote than ever.

Roger wondered where she went to every evening. He had even thought of following her, but in the end hadn't been able to bring himself to do it. He didn't think there was anyone else, but if there was he didn't want to know. Not yet, anyway.

He was sure everyone was right and that it was the accident and the loss of the baby that had caused Hilary to change. Roger thought back to the night of the accident: so much of it was hazy. He wished he could remember more. But there were only fragments of memory and they refused to come together even though he had spent hours trying to get them to form a clear picture.

He remembered the crash. And he thought he remembered Hilary calling out, while they were still in the car together.

And then there was the hideous scream that had seemed to go right through him. He knew that was Hilary and something to do with the baby. But there was nothing else. Except that when he had finally regained consciousness in the hospital there was a strange feeling about the whole place. And without being told, Roger knew it was something to do with Hilary and the baby.

He had tried asking the nurses and the doctor but they were their usual non-committal selves. There was just the remark by Dr Willis that perhaps the baby dying was all for the best. Why? What had been wrong with it?

Since the accident there had, of course, been other things. The storm and Hilary's intense sexual demands. The cat that had appeared so dramatically and that had seemed to threaten him. Where had it come from? Roger couldn't remember ever seeing anything like it before. And where had it gone? Their bedroom was on the top floor of the old Victorian house. It was a straight drop of over 70 feet to the small paved yard below. There wasn't a cat born that could survive a jump like that.

And after the storm there were all the other things. The sickness the following morning. The late night walks. The strange scene with the cat at Steve and Sue's. Why had that frightened him so?

Roger got up and poured himself a drink. The answer to everything seemed to be a cat, not the baby. He reached into the cupboard for a bottle of ginger ale only to find there wasn't any left, he'd have to have water. He was on his way to the kitchen when he remembered that there were half a dozen bottles of ginger ale in the sideboard in the dining room.

Roger put his whisky down on top of the sideboard and opened the right-hand door. He reached inside and took out a bottle. His right hand brushed against something hard. It was a book. Two books. What were they doing in here? Roger took them out and found himself looking into a pair of large green eyes that stared out at him from a wicked, whiskered, jet-black face.

He felt the sweat break out on his forehead. He dropped the books, reached for his whisky and gulped some down. His hand was shaking.

For a minute he could have sworn that it was the same face that had looked down at him from the window above the bed. Roger picked up the books and took them into the lounge. He supposed Hilary must have bought them or got them out of the library. He sat in his chair and started to leaf through the top book. Five pages in his eye was caught by a heading that read 'Pregnancy in cats'. The section was illustrated with pictures and diagrams. A line and wash drawing of a half-formed kitten in the womb seemed to jump off the page at Roger. He couldn't take his eyes off it. A thought started somewhere at the back of his head.

He took another drink. The thought was impossible. He was mad. But the idea wouldn't go away. And nor would the picture that accompanied it.

Roger shut the book, threw it and its companion to the floor. He had to talk to someone, but who? He finished his drink and poured himself another. He was drinking too much. He knew that, but it brought some comfort.

He thought about phoning his mother and father, but decided against it. They didn't seem to be interested in him or his problems at the moment. He'd popped in the other evening but he'd got the feeling they couldn't wait for him to go.

Roger looked at his watch. It was 11 o'clock. He wondered what time Hilary would get back. He decided to go to bed and try and get some sleep. His foot caught the book he'd thrown to the floor and it fell open at the page he'd been reading five minutes before.

Roger took one last look at the half-formed embryo of the cat and knew that the person he had to see was Dr Willis. Dr Willis knew the truth. And no matter how bad it was Roger wanted to know.

Carol Coren was fascinated by the death of Jean Merrow. She sat alone in front of the television set and watched and listened to every detail of the gruesome story. And there was more. Because if she was honest with herself then

Carol had to admit that the news of the second murder also excited her.

She was filled with a kind of expectancy. She knew that somehow she was involved, or was going to be involved.

Carol got up from her armchair and went to the window. She wondered if Hilary Wright would come. And if she'd heard the news. The bond between them was growing stronger. Carol could feel that. Mind you, that didn't mean she understood Hilary. She was a funny one, and no mistake.

She was determined to have a cat, set her heart on it. And there was nothing that her husband was going to be able to do about it. Hilary was a bit like a cat herself, Carol thought. Independent. And sensuous. Hilary prowled rather than walked.

Carol went and got some milk out of the fridge and took down two mugs from the kitchen cabinet. She was sure Hilary would come. Especially tonight when there was the murder to talk about. And they could have their cup of coffee together.

There was a ring on the bell. Carol felt a shock wave of excitement pass through her body, and hurried down the stairs to answer the door.

'Have you heard the news?' Carol asked even before Hilary had got her coat off.

'The death of the second nurse?'

'Yes. It's the same hospital, you know. The one you were in.'

Hilary nodded.

'Serve them right,' she said uncharacteristically. 'They killed my baby. I hope they all die.'

And that wasn't the only thing that Hilary said that evening that shocked Carol Coren.

Chapter Nine

Dr Willis hadn't wanted to see Roger Wright. These days he didn't want to see anyone. But in the end his professional training and a certain amount of curiosity had overcome his highly nervous state brought on by recent events and the effect of too many drugs combined with too much alcohol.

Now he was glad he'd agreed to the meeting. The young man was clearly in a disturbed state himself, and Dr Willis couldn't help wondering whether the cause of Roger's distress was the same as his own. There was also, although he didn't like to admit it, a small crumb of comfort in the young man's suffering.

Roger was shocked by Dr Willis's appearance. He had aged fifteen years since the accident. He'd lost weight too. And Roger thought his eyes looked funny, but he couldn't be sure. He also noticed that the doctor's hands were shaking badly. Roger put it down to overwork and the two murders. He had felt the gloomy atmosphere the minute he'd walked through the hospital entrance.

To start with the conversation had been almost casual. Dr Willis had asked Roger how he was, and how Hilary was feeling. Roger had answered briefly, and not at all truthfully, and hurried on to mention the recent events at the hospital. Dr Willis had agreed that the murders were terrible and that they had caused a lot of pain and extra work at the hospital.

There was a pause. And then Roger asked the question he'd come to ask.

'Dr Willis, after the baby died and before I saw my wife you said to me that maybe it was all for the best. That the baby had died, I mean. Why? What was wrong with it? I want to know.'

Roger's voice started to break.

'I take it your reason for asking is rather more urgent than just a wish to know?'

'Yes.'

'I'll answer your question in a minute, Mr Wright, but first could I ask you to tell me the reason? You see since the death of the . . .' Dr Willis hesitated, but then out of consideration for the young man opposite used the word he had automatically rejected, '. . . the child, strange things have been happening to me. And maybe to other people. Events that I've come to believe, against all my scientific training, are connected with that death.'

Roger didn't need any further encouragement to tell his story. For weeks now he'd kept his worries and his fears bottled up inside him, frightened that people would laugh at him, or tell him that he was going mad. But suddenly Roger knew that he wasn't mad, that the man, the doctor, sitting opposite him had suffered as he had. Roger told Dr Willis everything, starting with the scream in the hospital, right through to the discovery of the cat books in the dining room sideboard. It took over half an hour, and in all that time Dr Willis hardly moved a muscle.

'Is that it?' he asked when Roger stopped. 'You haven't left anything out?'

Roger hesitated. There was one thing. Only it wasn't fact, it was theory. His theory. Dr Willis waited.

'It's about the murder,' Roger blurted out.

'Yes,' Dr Willis almost snapped. And Roger could see that he had started to shake badly again.

'Well, I don't know how, but I think they've been done by some sort of cat . . . or cat person . . .'

Roger's voice died away. Now he'd said it out loud, the thought sounded ridiculous. He looked across the desk at Dr Willis expecting to see a smile on his face.

But the doctor wasn't smiling.

'What makes you say this?' he asked.

Roger shrugged. 'I don't know. Except that it's almost as if Hilary is becoming a cat or that she's . . . it sounds ridiculous, possessed by something, some animal.'

Roger looked down at the scratches on the back of his hand. They were like the marks from a cat's claw. 'I mean, the way the bodies were torn . . . it's like some huge cat, isn't it?'

Dr Willis nodded.

'Come with me,' he said getting up abruptly. 'I want to show you something.'

Roger followed Dr Willis along several hundred yards of corridor and up a floor to the pathology lab. From the minute he pushed his way through the swing door, Roger felt his eyes being drawn to the broken cupboard in the far corner of the room. He glanced at Dr Willis and received confirmation that the cupboard was what he'd been brought to see. Dr Willis led the way over to it. 'The child that you asked about was very unusual, Mr Wright. In all our years of medicine neither I nor Mr Stowell, the anaesthetist, had ever seen anything like it. It was so unusual that I took it upon myself to bring the foetus up here and lock it in this cupboard so that I could examine it at a later date.'

Roger cleared his throat nervously. 'What was it like?'

Dr Willis turned to face him. Roger could see he was reluctant to go further for fear of hurting his feelings.

'Look, I want to know. Really,' Roger almost whispered.

'Well, as I say, it was like no other baby I've ever seen. I can only describe it by saying it was a mixture of beings, half-human, half-animal.'

'Half-cat?' Roger asked.

'Yes. That's why I was so interested in what you had to say just now. It wasn't a very pretty sight, I'm afraid. The lower half was the human part of the baby. The upper half, the arms, certainly the head, were those of an unborn cat.'

Roger was silent for a moment. So that was what their child had looked like. He was about to ask another question when his eye was caught by a movement outside the window.

'Good Lord, look at that cat there,' he said.

Dr Willis did not look. Instead he asked, 'Is it black?'

'Yes. Why? Have you seen it before?'

'Yes.' There was something in Dr Willis's voice that made Roger look closely at him.

'Are you all right?' Roger asked.

'Let us go back to my office,' Dr Willis suggested. 'And I will explain. Including,' he added over his shoulder, 'the story of the broken cupboard.'

Back in the office, Dr Willis settled Roger in a chair with a cup of coffee and excused himself for five minutes, saying he had hospital business to attend to.

Roger had plenty to think about. He was frightened by what Dr Willis had told him. But he was also strangely relieved. He didn't understand what was happening, but he did understand that, at least, he was not going mad. And this thought, in the present dire circumstances, he found extremely comforting.

Dr Willis returned looking calmer. He had stopped shaking and seemed more in control of himself. Roger wondered if he'd nipped out for a quick drink. He wasn't too far from the truth. Dr Willis had used the five minute break to give himself another measured dose of morphine. He sat down in his big, old leather chair and started to tell Roger about the events of the last few weeks.

In the café in Station Road, Carol Coren was finding it hard to concentrate on her job. Three times already that morning she had taken orders to the wrong table. On the last occasion the customer had complained and the manageress had warned Carol to be more careful.

The trouble was she just couldn't forget what Hilary had told her last night. About the voice. And the things it told her to do.

Carol had been frightened at first, but then Hilary had explained that she, Carol, was going to be part of it too. And it seemed to make sense. Because that was what she'd felt all along. It was why she'd left Bill and come to live near Hilary. Hilary had told her she was going away for a day or two and that when she came back she would have the cat they'd talked about.

Carol had asked where she was going. And where she was going to get the cat from, but Hilary had said it was a secret. Well, all of it was secret, but that was particularly secret. Not that Hilary needed to worry. Carol hadn't understood all of it, but what she had, wild horses wouldn't have dragged out of her.

Roger didn't know what to say. Dr Willis had finished speaking two or three minutes before, but what he had said was still whirling round Roger's brain. It was fantastic. Even more fantastic than he had dared to think about. Surely they had got it wrong. Roger went over to the window, and moved the blind. The cat was there, just as Dr Willis had said it would be. And Roger could feel the quiet menace it directed toward Dr Willis. And himself.

'What can we do?' he asked.

'Nothing, Mr Wright. We are helpless. We cannot change fate. I don't know how many times this has happened, there is so much mystery. But Bast, the cat-goddess, certainly dates back as far as the Second Dynasty in Egyptian Mythology.'

Dr Willis stood up, and joined Roger at the window. He had a strange smile on his face. 'In that time who can say how many times this cycle of rebirth both as a human and as a cat has taken place. Or how many humans have had to die to make the rebirth of Ra come to pass, perfectly. Perhaps you will survive. She may have a purpose for you. But I have failed and I know I must die. Quite soon, I think.'

As he finished speaking Dr Willis released the blind and stood facing the sleek, black cat out of the window. Somehow the conversation with Roger had brought to him a final acceptance of the fate he knew was in store.

He stood at the window a long time, trying to understand this creature who sat opposite him. But the animal gave nothing, moved not one long, black whisker. Roger left with a muttered, 'Goodbye' that he was sure Dr Willis hadn't heard.

Outside the sky was grey and overcast. Roger shivered in the chill of the east wind that had sprung up. And from the new knowledge he had gained from Dr Willis.

He stood on the pavement looking left and right, not sure what to do. He couldn't face going to the office. And he certainly didn't want to go home to Hilary. He needed time to sort out his thoughts.

There was a café fifty yards down on the left from the hospital. And suddenly it looked warm and inviting. It seemed as good a place as any to Roger to sit and try and sort out a few of his problems.

The café was busy. Quite a few of the people looked as if they had just come from a hospital visit.

Roger chose a small table at the back of the café. It was good to be out of the wind. He looked at the badly typed menu and ordered a black coffee and a toasted bacon sandwich.

A young boy of about 17 brought him his order. The coffee was hot and as Roger sipped it, he could almost forget the horror of what was happening to him.

He was brought back to earth by the appearance of a

sleek Siamese cat that prowled between the legs of the café chairs and tables like some big cat in the jungle.

Roger watched the cat approach. It was making straight for him. He felt his hands begin to shake. He put down the coffee cup. The Siamese stopped by the side of Roger's table and sat looking up at him. Roger could feel his legs shaking now. He wanted to leave. To run out of the place, but he couldn't move.

He could feel his stomach churning over, the fear spreading through him, affecting the whole chemistry of his body. He felt the bile rise to his throat. He was going to be sick. And then to his shame he felt his bowels move. And he knew he had dirtied himself.

He lashed out with his foot at the cat. And it ran off through the tables. The proprietor looked up and started to call out something, angrily. But Roger didn't hear what he said. He pulled on his coat and ran out of the café and down the road.

He ran for quite a while. His heart thumping, his whole body shaking with fright and with shame. A mile down the road he saw a cab and hailed it. The driver looked at him suspiciously and seemed reluctant to accept the fare. Roger wondered if he could smell the mess in his trousers.

He made up a story about coming from the hospital where his wife was dying, and the cab driver seemed to relax. Sitting in the cab, with the window half-open, Roger found himself wishing the story was true. And then immediately felt a stab of pain as he remembered how good it had been between Hilary and himself before the accident.

He paid off the cab and walked slowly up the short garden path. He felt himself beginning to shake again. He didn't know how to face Hilary. What to say to her. What to do. His hands were shaking so badly that it took him two or three minutes to open the front door.

Roger stood on the step, listening at the open door.

The house was quiet. He called out, 'Hilary!'

There was no answer. He waited a minute and then called out again. Louder this time. Someone passing in the street looked at him queerly.

There was no answer from inside the house. Roger felt calmer. He went into the house and shut the front door behind him. There was a letter in the kitchen. On the table. It was brief and to the point. It was signed Hilary. Not love Hilary, just Hilary.

She was visiting Aunt Joan for a few days and didn't know when she'd be back. Roger was not to get in touch. He went up to the bathroom, ripped off his soiled clothing and ran himself a hot bath. The panic had passed away and Roger let himself dream of pleasant things as he lay cocooned in the warmth of the water.

It wasn't until he went back downstairs to make himself a cup of coffee that he read the note again. It was quite clear. And very unlike Hilary. Roger shrugged his shoulders. Maybe Aunt Joan had returned early. Or maybe Hilary just wanted to be alone. Or, then again, maybe she was somewhere else all together. Perhaps with someone else.

Roger sat thinking about the last possibility. He didn't think it was likely, especially in view of what he'd learnt from Dr Willis, but it would explain some things.

For a moment Roger found himself hoping that it was just another man. Even if it was the end between Hilary and himself. At least that way he wouldn't have to live with the fears and suspicions that Dr Willis had seemed to turn into a fantastic certainty.

The phone rang and Roger stood in front of it trembling, unwilling to pick it up in case it was Hilary. It continued to ring. Roger moved forward and picked up the receiver as carefully as if it was the trigger of a loaded revolver.

It was Steve wanting to know where he was. There was

a panic in the agency. A new business pitch that needed working on overnight. Roger made his excuses and was aware of the distinct lack of sympathy at the other end of the phone.

He knew he was pushing his luck with the agency. The accident had been some time ago now. And people's memories were short. But how could he explain? And if he did, who would believe him. He felt trapped.

Roger went into the lounge and poured himself a brandy to go with his coffee. He sat hunched up over the kitchen table trying to decide what to do. But all he could think of was Dr Willis and the story of Bast, the cat-goddess.

After another brandy, he decided to search the house and in particular those parts of it where Hilary kept her papers and her private things. Maybe somewhere there was a clue that would prove something, one way or another.

What he found was in the cellar. And there was something else, in Hilary's underwear drawer. The something else was a book. Quite big and lavishly illustrated, it was on Egyptian Mythology. Roger sat on the bed and flicked over the pages. There were pictures of early Egyptian gods. Half-human, half-animal. Horus, with his falcon's head, Thoth with the head of a dog, Set with the head of the Typhonian animal and more, many more. Serpents, crocodiles, goats, calves, the Ichnewnon, Alion, Alyma.

And cats! Bast!

Roger read the caption printed below a picture of two mummified cats.

'Honoured in death, the bodies of cats were frequently embalmed, mummified and buried with all the pomp accorded in human rites.'

The picture was credited to the British Museum. As were others in the book.

Roger put the book back where he'd found it and went downstairs with a feeling of unease. On the kitchen table, where he'd left them, were the things he'd found in a lined box in the cellar.

He picked up the black, jewelled cat collar and examined it more closely. It was a beautiful piece of work. He wondered where Hilary had found it, or had it made. There was a small silver name tag by the ornate bauble. On it was inscribed the name, Ra. Roger turned it over and saw his own address and telephone number on the back.

He put the collar back in the box and picked up a small silver feeding bowl. It too had the name Ra on the back.

It was a name Roger recognized. He had just read it, upstairs in the book on Egyptian Mythology. Phrases came drifting back to him.

'Ra was called the father of the Gods . . .

. . . it was thought he rose from the primeval waters enclosed within the petals of a lotus blossom, which enfolded him once more when he returned to it each night . . .

. . . the tears were shed by Ra's Eye, whose peculiarity was that it was separate from him and had a mind of its own . . .

. . . Ra wore the double crown of Egypt which combined the red crown of Lower Egypt and the white crown of Upper Egypt. As on the crown of the Pharaohs, the serpent was seen at the front rearing its head and spitting fire at all enemies.'

And there was more. Much, much more. But Roger couldn't remember it. Didn't want to remember it. And what he could remember, he desperately wanted to forget.

But the last thing he'd read seemed to fill his mind. It was about Ra in his form as a cat and how a wife, Bast, was selected for him. After his union with her, she bore him a son who in time fertilized his own mother, and was reborn as his own son.

Bast was a goddess in her own right and one much revered as the consort of Ra and mother of a mighty God-King. According to legend she could take either human or animal form as well as her traditional one. For Ra to be reborn as his own son the cycle had to be completed in both forms.

Roger didn't know where Hilary had gone. He was sure she wasn't at her Aunt Joan's. He was also sure, now, that when she returned she would not be alone.

Chapter Ten

It was the way in which Albert Stowell died that at first led the police to believe that this murder was unconnected with those of Helen Champion and Jean Merrow.

True, Albert worked at St Michael's Hospital, amongst others, but there were no claw marks, no ripped flesh and the deceased was not an attractive young nurse.

When Mrs Stowel had left to go to the shops, Mr Stowell had been reading the paper in the breakfast room. When she had returned, he was in the same old easy chair, but he was dead. Suffocation was the official verdict.

Other than that, there was nothing to go on. Except for a few cat hairs on the collar of his shirt and on the front of his waistcoat.

It was Sergeant Childs who first pointed out that cat hair had been found on the clothing of Helen Champion. And on the bedroom floor of Jean Merrow's flat.

At the time no-one had thought to ask the next-of-kin, neighbours, friends of the two nurses if they'd owned a cat. As it turned out they hadn't. And neither had Mr and Mrs Stowell.

At first the police had not been sure whether Albert Stowell's death was murder. There was little sign of a struggle. And no sign at all of anyone having broken into the house. Or of anything being taken.

But the pathologist had been adamant. Death had been caused by suffocation. And that had required a certain amount of outside force or pressure that the dead man could not have applied himself.

And there was, of course, the expression on the dead

man's face. It was not one that Sergeant Childs wanted to see again. A mixture of incredulity and sheer terror.

And that was what Albert Stowell had felt as he'd died. He had been sitting reading *The Guardian* when he had heard a noise in the kitchen. He had gone out to investigate and to his surprise had found a marmalade-coloured cat sitting in the middle of the red, tiled floor.

Albert Stowell didn't particularly like cats, but the creature had looked so pathetic sitting there that he had scooped it up and taken it back into the breakfast room with him.

Perhaps he'd give it some milk later, when Marjorie got back from the shops. Albert picked up his paper and started to read again. The cat sat on the Chinese rug and watched him, silently.

Albert forgot the cat was there until it jumped up on to his lap. It felt heavy for such a little thing. Albert put the paper to one side and got the shock of his life.

He wanted to shout out, but the words seemed to stick in his throat. He tried to get up. Fought to get up, but the weight and size of the thing that was sitting on him was too much.

It started to move up his body, its bright eyes never leaving his face.

'Why?' Albert asked helplessly.

The huge thing seemed to grin at him. Albert could feel its breath on his face. And then its fur in his mouth and up his nostrils. And eventually over his eyes, like some heavy, furry cushion obliterating the light.

Albert couldn't breathe. He struggled and he fought, but the thing was too strong for him. He felt himself slipping away. He tried to gasp for air, but he couldn't open his mouth. He knew he was dying. And suddenly at the last moment he knew why.

The foetus!

That was why! And it was as Albert understood this, that the thing on his lap began to laugh.

Carol Coren heard about the murder on the news. And immediately thought of Hilary. She didn't particularly think of Hilary as the person responsible for the murder, but through the news of the murder, somehow she knew that Hilary had returned. She picked up the phone and dialled Hilary's number.

Ten minutes later, full of excitement, Carol was on her way round to Hilary's house. Hilary had got it! And she, Carol Coren, was going to be the first person to see it.

Roger had called in to see his mother. He was worried about her. In the last few weeks, since the accident, she had changed out of all recognition. And so for that matter had his father.

They seemed happy enough. Very happy, in fact. But there was something funny about it all. For instance his mother had taken to wearing clothes that Roger did not think were suitable for a woman of her age.

And they were always out. Or else they simply didn't answer the phone. Roger had rung several times when he was sure they must be in, but there was no reply.

And once, when he'd called round on the off chance, they hadn't answered the door. Although the lights were on and he was sure he could hear voices inside the house.

'Here you are, dear, have a nice cup of tea. You're sure you wouldn't prefer something stronger?'

'No thanks, Mother.'

'I think I'll have a sherry myself,' his mother said and poured herself a Harvey's Bristol Cream. 'You look tired, dear,' she said as she sat down on the settee next to Roger.

Roger looked down at his cup and saucer and noticed in

the process that the slit in his mother's skirt revealed a long length of black stocking.

'Mother,' Roger said, carefully. 'I want to talk to you about . . .'

Judith Wright looked at her watch and jumped up. 'Excuse me a minute, dear. I want to hear the news,' she said and went over to the radio and switched it on.

It was the first item on the news. Roger sat white-faced listening to the, as yet, sparse details. His teacup started to rattle on the saucer. And his mother reached over and took them away from him.

'Drink this, dear,' she said, handing him a strong brandy and soda.

Roger gulped at the drink and sat staring at the little radio on the book shelf opposite him.

'They seem to be having a lot of trouble at that hospital of yours,' his mother said.

Roger nodded, but he wasn't really listening. He was thinking. About Hilary. She was back.

He knew it!

He finished off his drink and got up to go. He'd meant to tell his mother all about it, what Dr Willis had told him, everything. He had to talk to someone. But the moment had gone. And anyway, now he thought about it, he doubted that she'd have understood. He sent his love to his father and left to go home. Home to Hilary and he wasn't sure what else.

After he'd gone, Judith Wright had spent some time thinking about her son. She hadn't forgotten her fears at the time of the accident. They were still with her. But she knew she couldn't do anything about them. She knew that what was going to happen, had to happen. And that somehow her new-found relationship with Lionel was all part of it.

It was as if whatever was threatening Roger, was also compensating her, and Lionel, for the pain it was going to inflict on him. She looked at her watch: Lionel would be home soon. She looked at herself in the hall mirror, and undid another button on her blouse.

Roger let himself into the house and stood quietly in the hall. Hilary's coat was draped over the newel post at the foot of the stairs. The sight of it made him feel uneasy. He checked the downstairs rooms, but they were empty. He stared up the stairs, cautiously. Not quite knowing what to expect or why he was so nervous. As he reached the landing he heard voices coming from the nursery. Laughter too.

Roger stood outside the nursery door, listening. He could hear Hilary's voice. And another, a woman's voice, but he did not recognize it.

He turned the handle of the door and pushed open a gap of about two inches. Through the gap he could see Hilary and the other woman kneeling on the floor in front of the cot he and Hilary had bought for the baby. The two of them were playing with something between the bars.

Roger pushed the door open fully and went inside. The two women looked round at him. Hilary seemed unconcerned, but the other was nervous, and Roger guessed that Hilary had told her at least some of their troubles.

But it was not Hilary or her friend that Roger was looking at. There was something else, in the cot. A small, ebony black kitten with the brightest and the largest green eyes Roger had ever seen.

Roger looked at the cat. The cat looked at Roger. It was as if they were weighing each other up for the battle that both knew was to come. Hilary broke the silence.

'Hello, darling. Come and meet Carol. Carol, this is my husband Roger. Roger, this is Carol Coren, a friend of mine.'

Roger shook Carol's hand and said, 'Hello.'

'And this,' Hilary went on, 'this is Ra. Or, to give him his full title, Prince Ra.'

'Where did you get him?' Roger asked rudely.

Hilary ignored the question. 'I'm sure you two are going to be great friends,' she went on. 'Aren't you, Ra darling,' she added, stroking the kitten with her finger.

'He's not staying,' Roger said.

Carol shifted uneasily and started to get up.

'Don't be silly, darling. Of course he is. This is his home now, isn't it Ra?' She kissed the kitten through the bars of the cot. Then added, 'Carol's going to stay and have something to eat with us, aren't you Carol?'

Carol looked uncomfortable. 'Well, I don't know, I mean . . .'

'Of course you will, we'll go and see what there is in a minute. And you can see Ra have his tea.'

'I'm going out,' Roger said and left the room slamming the door behind him.

'It's Roger,' Sue said with her hand over the phone.

'What's he want?' Steve asked.

'To speak to you, silly.'

'Tell him I've gone out to the pub, or something.'

Sue glared at him and started on a long story about how he'd been here a minute ago, but that now she couldn't find him anywhere and that he must have gone down to the pub. It didn't sound very convincing. But Steve didn't care.

Sue put the phone down. 'Why didn't you want to speak to him?' she demanded.

'Because I've had enough of him for the minute.'

'Poor Roger. I'm sure he guessed. He sounded very down. I wonder what's happened now.'

Steve snorted. 'There isn't much more left to happen. The bloke's losing his marbles. You should hear some of the stuff he comes out with. You don't know the half of it.'

Sue went over and put her arms round Steve. 'It's not

like you to get so upset. You've worked with Roger a long time now.'

Steve shrugged. 'It'll be all right, I expect. I mean the guy's just not pulling his weight at the moment. He's never there when you want him. I'm working with two other writers at the moment, because he can't get himself together.'

'Perhaps I should go over and see Hilary,' Sue suggested. 'And see if I can find out what's the matter.'

'I'd stay well out of it if I were you. Something funny's happening between those two and they'll have to sort it out.'

Carol Coren had left by the time Roger got back to the house. He had gone to the pub for a drink and then to the 'Light of India' curry house next door to Panny's, in the High Street.

He was the only person in the place and Roger had used the peace and quiet to calm himself down and think about what he was going to do next.

He realized he had been silly to storm out of the house like that. He had to talk to Hilary. And it wasn't going to help if he made scenes in front of her friends. Roger wondered who Carol Coren was. She was not much older than Hilary, and even more shy than Hilary had been when Roger had first met her. The two of them certainly seemed to get on together. They were more like a couple of sisters than friends. And it was all so sudden. Perhaps Hilary liked her because Carol liked cats. Roger wished he did. Particularly this one. But he didn't. And in those first few seconds when they'd looked at each other, Roger knew that the cat had recognized the fact. And had challenged him to do something about it.

Well, he would do something about it. He would do something that neither Hilary, nor the cat, would expect. He would learn to like the wretched animal. Maybe then there would be an end to the miserable business. Maybe the killing would stop. And they could all live together, happily, like he and Hilary had before.

Hilary was in bed when Roger got home. She was reading. The book on Egyptian Mythology Roger had found in her drawer. He got himself undressed and went into the bathroom to wash and clean his teeth. He wished now he hadn't had a curry: garlic always seemed to stay on his breath for ages.

Roger turned off the bathroom light and walked back to the bedroom. He paused outside the half-open door of the nursery and looked in. A pair of large green eyes stared back at him through the bars of the cot. They made Roger feel uncomfortable. He felt his stomach contract and a nervous excitement run through his body.

He went into the bedroom. Hilary was still reading.

'I'm sorry about earlier,' Roger said, hanging up his dressing gown.

'It's all right,' Hilary answered without lifting her eyes from her book.

'He's quite a sweet little chap really,' Roger went on. 'I've just been in to see him.'

'Yes.'

'How old is he?' Roger asked.

'A few weeks.'

'He's very small.'

'He'll grow quite quickly, now.'

Roger nodded without quite understanding the emphasis Hilary put on the words, and picked up the previous week's colour supplement from the *Sunday Times*. He was half way through an article on Victorian painters.

'Will he be all right in the nursery?' Roger asked. 'I mean, what if he wants to go to the loo or something?'

Hilary put her book down. 'He's house-trained. You don't have to worry. Anyway he can climb out of there if he wants to, he did earlier when Carol was here.'

Roger put down the colour supplement and turned towards Hilary. She looked very beautiful. He put his hand out and touched her arm. She didn't seem to mind.

'Where did you go, Hilary?' Roger asked gently. 'I was worried.'

'You needn't have been. I was all right. I had to go and get Ra.'

Roger wanted to ask where that was, but he sensed that too many questions would not help him re-establish the relationship he wanted back so badly.

He turned out the light on his side of the bed, then turned to face Hilary, and to his surprise found that she was facing him. Roger put out an arm and Hilary moved close to him. Her body felt soft and yielding. Roger started to stroke her thigh with his hand. Gently, he kissed her cheek. And then her lips. Hilary kissed him back and they stayed very close to one another for several minutes.

Roger moved his hand up and started to stroke Hilary's breast. He felt the nipple stiffen at his touch. He felt Hilary's arm move and a moment later her hand started to stroke him.

They kissed again. Hilary rolled over on to her back pulling Roger on top of her.

'Come on, come on,' she whispered urgently in his ear.

'Oh Hilary,' Roger whispered and began to enter her.

The scream came from next door. The nursery. It was a high-pitched sound that sent a shiver of fear through Roger's body. Hilary broke away, jumped out of bed and ran to the nursery.

A minute later she came back clutching Ra to her naked body. 'It's all right, Mummy's here,' she whispered to the animal and stroked its head with her hand. She got back into bed, still holding the cat, still caressing it, still whispering comfort in its ear.

Roger felt the animal looking at him and turned to meet its gaze. There was a look of triumph on its face. Roger could almost hear it say, 'You won't beat me.' He turned over and tried to get to sleep, but he felt tense and frustrated.

Hilary settled Ra down on the duvet beside her. After a minute or two Roger put out his hand and touched her breast, but she moved away with a whispered, 'No, Roger. Not now.'

It was late when Carol Coren turned out her bedroom light. She had been reading the book Hilary had lent her. It was about the gods of Ancient Egypt and the mysteries of the Pyramids. She had read the chapters on Ra and Bast several times to make sure she understood them. And could remember them.

Now she lay with the sheet and blankets almost over her head thinking about what she'd read. And about what Hilary had told her over supper. It would certainly be nice to live in that house with a room of her own.

She'd enjoy looking after Ra. And the baby, except that as the doctors had told Hilary she couldn't have any more children, Carol didn't quite see where the baby was going to come from.

There was also Hilary's insistence that she might have to help Mr Wright. Carol didn't understand that. But then there were a lot of things that Hilary said, and did, that Carol didn't understand. Well, not in the proper sense. She just knew that what Hilary said would happen, would happen.

Just like Ra had happened. And Mr Wright had been cross, but it would be all right in the end. Carol was glad she'd got Hilary for a friend. It was as if they'd known each other for ages. Funny how Hilary's father had been called Derek too.

* * *

Roger did not sleep well. The presence of the cat and Hilary's fussing over it kept him awake for long periods of the night. Thoughts that he'd been eager to put aside just a few hours before came flooding back into his head. The cat wasn't just a cat. It had a mind of its own. It was an intelligent being. Roger could feel and see it thinking. And its aim was to take over his relationship with Hilary.

Dr Willis had been right. They were dealing with something that was way beyond them. But despite that, surely there was something they could do to stop it. Roger decided he would ring Dr Willis in the morning and try to persuade him to help.

The morning was wet and grey. The sky seemed threatening. And the atmosphere in the house was not friendly. Hilary busied herself with Ra, leaving Roger to get his own breakfast.

This he did with difficulty, managing to burn the toast and break a teacup in the process. And after each mishap he could feel the cat looking at him, gloating, waiting for him to make another mistake.

Roger left the house as soon as he could, saying that he might be late home. An announcement that did not seem to worry Hilary. It wasn't until he was on the tube that Roger realized something else that was strange about the scene he had left behind. Ra had grown during the night. Quite considerably.

There were several panics at the agency and it was twelve-thirty before Roger could phone the hospital. Steve had gone out to get some sandwiches so they could work through lunch, which meant Roger had the office to himself for ten minutes.

He dialled the number and waited for what seemed like ages before getting an answer.

'Could I speak to Dr Willis, please.'

'Dr Willis's office.'

'Is he there, please?'

'I'm sorry Dr Willis is away on sick leave at present. Can anyone else help?'

'No . . . thank you. Can you tell me when you expect him back?'

'I'm afraid we don't have a date at present. Dr Cochrane is dealing with all his work, can I put you through to him?'

'No, thank you,' Roger said and put down the receiver.

He had wanted to ask where Dr Willis was, if he was at home, but the cold efficient voice at the other end of the phone had stopped him. Roger knew now that he was on his own. If there was anything that could be done, he would have to do it.

Dr Willis was at home. He had left the house only briefly over the last two days, to get fresh supplies of alcohol and tobacco. The little food he ate he got from the well stocked deep-freeze.

He had lost weight and his hair was starting to fall out. There were other signs too that the mixture of drugs and alcohol was affecting his body, as well as his mind.

Most of the time he slept in his favourite armchair. Slept and dreamed. And in amongst the dreams was the nightmare. The nightmare he knew was destined to become reality. And he would wake, screaming. And shaking, sweat running down his face and his body. And then, his hands shaking, he would get himself another drink, or another dose of drugs and let his mind wander off on some new path.

Chapter Eleven

Ian Wert was sorry he'd come now. He'd only agreed to see the surgeon to please his mother. And then, when the day had finally arrived, she'd talked him into keeping the appointment.

Anyway, he'd got used to his face the way it was. And so, for that matter, had all his mates. Scarface, they called him. Like the American gangster.

And it certainly didn't seem to have put the birds off. They were queuing up to take a tumble with him. There was a new one every night.

And now there was this toffee-nosed bloke poking around his face and asking questions. Had he had any trouble with the scars since the accident? Ian said, no. There'd been that bleeding on the night of the storm but it had cleared up on its own.

There were more questions about the accident and the treatment he'd received at St Michael's.

The doctor raised his eyes at the mention of the hospital. But Ian was used to that. It had become a joke that the accident had turned him into a maniac and that it was him doing all the murders, to get his own back. That girl the other night looked as if she believed it. But it didn't stop her coming across a bit later.

The examination ended and the doctor told Ian that he'd be in touch. He could certainly do something, but he couldn't promise to cover all the scars.

Sue hadn't told Steve she was going to see Hilary. He hadn't sounded too keen when she'd suggested it the night before, so she'd waited until he'd left for work and then rung and arranged to arrive about eleven, in time for coffee.

The cat had been a surprise. But apart from that Hilary seemed fine. Sue wondered why Roger had sounded so upset on the phone the previous evening. Perhaps Steve was right and he really was cracking up.

Certainly Hilary had gone a little overboard on the cat. What was its name? Ra. But then perhaps that was only to be expected after losing the baby.

And if Roger was behaving strangely and coming up with wild ideas all over the place, then it was probably a good idea that Hilary did have something else to interest herself in.

When she'd talked about the awful murders at the hospital, Hilary had seemed genuinely frightened. And Sue had made a note to tell Roger to be more careful about what he said, when she next saw him.

Sue had finally left about 1 o'clock, having refused lunch because she had the shopping to do. And when she left she was quite sure in her mind that there was nothing wrong with Hilary Wright. Nothing at all.

Roger's day at the office had not been an easy one. He'd had so much time off recently and there seemed to be problems on all of the accounts he worked on with Steve.

And on top of it all the Carter's Cake client had suddenly demanded a late meeting that would probably end in them all having to go out to dinner.

Roger rang Hilary and told her he would be late. She reminded him that he'd already warned her before he left for work. He asked about her day but didn't succeed in getting much of a reply. He asked after Ra, and detected a little more warmth at the other end of the phone.

The meeting ended at 8 o'clock and as Roger had guessed, Clive Walker, the Carter's Cake Marketing Manager, suggested they all went out for something to eat. He was on the sleeper to Newcastle and was at a loose end up till 11.30 P.M. Roger thought about making his excuses, but a warning look from Steve made him think better of it.

It was midnight before he got home. The lights were out in the lounge and Roger guessed that Hilary had gone to bed. He let himself into the hall quietly, and started to creep up the stairs.

It was then he heard it. A soft moaning sound coming from the bedroom. It was Hilary's voice, husky and low, calling out like she did when they made love.

Roger grabbed hold of the banister rail to steady himself. He couldn't believe it. Not Hilary. Not here in their house, in their bed! For a minute Roger was tempted to run out of the house, but then anger, fuelled by the whisky and the wine he'd drunk with dinner, took over.

He thrust open the bedroom door and saw Hilary's face caught in a shaft of moonlight that had spilt its way through a gap in the curtains. She lay on top of the bed, naked. Her whole body seemed alive, moving as if in some erotic dance.

On top of her lay a black shape that seemed to move with her.

Roger snapped on the light.

'Hilary!' he shouted.

Hilary opened her eyes, and then closed them again, immediately, against the brightness of the light.

'Roger, what's the matter?' she asked. 'I was asleep.'

Roger looked at her. The black shape that had seemed so much like a man a minute ago was smaller. And black and furry. It was Ra.

Roger marched over to the bed. 'It's disgusting!' he shouted and flung the cat from the bed.

Hilary sat up, angry. 'You're mad,' she said. And then looked at him more closely. 'Have you been drinking again?' she accused.

Roger looked angry. 'I thought you had someone with you . . . that you were . . . well, you were calling out like you used to when we made love.'

Hilary got out of bed and put on a black negligee that Roger had given her at Christmas.

'You need to see a doctor,' she said over her shoulder as she bent to pick up the cat.

'Come on, Ra. Come to Mummy,' she crooned. 'We'll sleep in the nursery tonight, away from the horrid man.'

Roger watched her leave the room, the cat cradled in her arms. He couldn't see the cat's face, but he knew that there was a smile on it.

Roger lay in bed replaying the scene he had walked in on earlier, over and over again in his mind. He knew that it was Ra on the bed with Hilary, he had proved it for himself when he turned on the light. But he still couldn't rid himself of the feeling that she had been making love with a man when he had first entered the bedroom.

Maybe, ridiculous as it sounded, the cat had the power to transform itself into human shape. Roger was certain that it could think like a human and transmit those thoughts when it wanted to.

Certainly Dr Willis had believed that the cat-goddess, Bast, had magical powers. Maybe if he could find out more there would be a way to stop all of the strange things that were happening. Maybe, Roger thought, he could get rid of Ra.

The thought had hardly entered his mind when he heard or thought he heard, from the other room a laugh that seemed to mock him. A laugh that seemed to say, try it if you dare.

'So who's going to be a pretty boy, then?' Frankie Hardy teased after Ian Wert had finished telling them all about his visit to the plastic surgeon.

They were all in the Green King, Charlie, Bill, Alan,

Dave, Fred, and their various ladies. It was where they started every evening, over a few pints.

'I don't think I'll bother,' Ian replied. 'I'm doing all right as I am.' He leered at Sally.

'Aren't I, darling?' he asked.

Sally giggled and the others joined in. Ian's comments didn't go unnoticed. Ian saw another girl, further along the bar, laughing too. He'd seen her earlier. She was on her own, and he'd supposed she was waiting for someone. Tasty little number, she was. And she was still on her own. He smiled at her and she smiled back.

Ian nudged Dave Clark and whispered something in his ear. A minute later Dave announced he was going to the gents. His route took him past the girl further down the bar. He reached the door of the gents and nodded to Ian. It meant that the girl was alone and from the grin on Dave's face the rest of her matched up to her very attractive face with its frame of jet black hair.

Dave waited for five minutes inside the lavatory and then came back again. On his way through he stopped and spoke to the girl. She looked across at the group, looked at her watch and then nodded.

'She's going to give 'im five more minutes and if 'e 'asn't come by then, she'll come over,' he said in reply to Ian's question. 'Now I reckon that deserves another bleeding pint.'

Ian ordered a fresh round of drinks. He could have asked the girl over himself, but since the accident he liked to give them a bit of time to get used to the face. For a lot of them it was a proper turn-on, but there were one or two who'd backed away a bit sharpish. And it got to him.

He paid for the drinks and turned back to the group just as the girl arrived. She was a proper cracker and no mistake. Great long legs, big tits and a tiny waist. Her name was Angela and Ian bought her a snowball and started talking to Charlie Stevens. He could hear the girls chatting to the new bird in the background. Give them five minutes and they'd know everything there was to know about her, then he'd move in a bit.

But it didn't quite work out like that, because several other mates arrived and someone started playing the juke box and somehow whenever Ian tried to get next to Angela, someone else was already there giving her the old bunny.

At ten o'clock Peter Jenks suggested that as there weren't any parties that sounded any good, they have one of their own.

There was a lot of discussion about where to have it until Sandra announced that her parents were away for the weekend. And that seemed to settle it. There was a mass exodus from the pub with everyone clutching bottles and cans and packets of crisps.

Ian had meant to offer Angela a lift to Worple Road, but when he looked around she'd already gone. Maybe she wasn't going to the party. Shame, a sexy bird like that, still never mind, there were plenty of others around.

It was a good party. Plenty of beers and the odd bottle of scotch and vodka. And some good music. People kept on arriving and others kept disappearing either upstairs or out into the yard.

Sandra kept telling everyone to be careful and saying how they'd all have to come round the next day and help her clear up.

Ian had been there an hour when he saw Angela. And she was on her own! Blimey, wonders would never cease!

'You're Ian, aren't you?' she asked.

'Yeah. Only they call me scarface now on account of this,' he said pointing to his face.

Angela put out a hand and touched his right cheek. Her fingers traced their way down a thin pink scar.

'Doesn't it hurt?' she asked.

'Naw, not any more.'

'How did it happen?'

Ian told her about the accident.

'What about the others?' she asked. 'The man and his wife?'

'Don't know,' he lied. 'Someone said he'd been nicked by the police. Something to do with those murders at the 'ospital, but they let 'im go. What about you?' Ian asked. 'Where do you come from?'

Angela shrugged and gave a funny little smile. 'Around.'

'What were you doing in that pub this evening?'

'I'd arranged to meet someone only they didn't show up.'

''e must be barmy standing up a smashing looking doll like you.'

'Who said it was a man?' she asked.

'It was, wasn't it?'

'Never you mind. Why don't you ask me to dance?' she said, nodding her head in the direction of several other couples who had started dancing to the music coming from Sandra's music centre.

They danced quite a while before Angela said she was hot and that she was going out into the yard for some fresh air.

Ian went with her and it wasn't long before they were huddled up close and kissing away.

Ian moved his arm down and started to run his hand over Angela's breasts. She didn't seem to mind. He pulled up the bottom of her sweater and sneaked his hand underneath. Her flesh seemed to be alive. She wasn't wearing a bra. Her breasts were large and her nipples seemed to grow by the minute.

Ian could feel her tongue working feverishly in his mouth. And he felt himself getting very excited. Her hand touched the fly of his trousers and started to stroke him. Jesus, she was dynamite. He took his hand down from her sweater and slid it up the long split in the side of her skirt. Flesh. Smooth and firm. And eager. And, Christ, nothing else. She wasn't wearing a thing under that skirt.

His hand worked its way between her long legs and his fingers touched the mass of fine silky hair. Angela pulled away from him.

'Oh no! You're not one of those!' Ian accused.

'No, I am not one of those,' Angela replied coldly. 'I'm as worked up as you are, and I'd like to go on. But one, I'm cold and two, I'm not putting on a performance for anyone who cares to wander out here. Right?'

'What'cha want to do?' Ian asked. 'I've got the car, we could use that.'

Angela looked unimpressed. 'And three, I gave up doing it in cars years ago,' she said.

Ian was silent. Bloody women, she would be awkward, he thought. He'd got a good mind to tell her to get lost. But, Christ, she was hot stuff and he knew that he wouldn't be satisfied with anyone else on this particular night. Who did he know who had a flat or a room he could use? He was going to have to get a place of his own.

The Greenes! They were away on some sort of late holiday. He remembered his mother talking about it. They'd asked her to pop in a couple of times during the fortnight and see if everything was all right in their precious house. Stuck-up lot! Ian laughed out loud at the thought of seeing Angela in old man Greene's bed!

'You sound happy all of a sudden?' Angela said.

'Yeah, I am,' Ian leered. 'Cracked it, 'aven't I? Come on.'

She pulled him closer to her and kissed him, at the same time undoing the zip of his trousers. Ian felt her strong hands seek out his now excited phallus. She ran her nails lightly down the outside of his hardness. The shock ran right through his body, for a moment he thought he was going to come.

‘Who’s a big boy then,’ she whispered. And then drew away from him with a laugh as he started to thrust himself against her.

Ian did up his fly. ‘You wait,’ he said. ‘You just bloody wait.’

They slipped away from the party, unseen. Angela waited in the car while Ian went into his house and got the key to the Greenes’. He’d been worried when he’d told her where they were going that she wouldn’t play along. But she hadn’t seemed to mind. She’d been all over him on the journey home. Touching him everywhere, until he’d had to tell her to lay off, or he’d crash the car.

And that was funny. He hadn’t really thought about the accident while driving until tonight. Then, just for a minute he’d felt frightened. But the knowledge of what was to come quickly drove the fear from his mind.

Ian left the car two or three doors up from the Greenes’. The road was deserted. They walked quietly up the path and slipped in through the front door.

She was at him the minute he’d closed the door. First his jacket came off then his shirt, almost ripped from his back.

After that he started in on his own account. By the time they reached the top of the stairs they were both naked. They stumbled and rolled into the Greenes’ bedroom. The moon seemed very bright and cast a golden, almost luminous glow over the bed.

For the first time since they’d taken their clothes off, they could see each other. Ian couldn’t stop looking at Angela. Her figure was perfect. She looked like some statue, or a painting he’d seen in a magazine or book.

She made him lay on the bed and then started to slowly lick him all over. Ian’s skin jumped at the touch of her tongue. It was as if the whole surface of his body was alive with tiny electrical currents.

Her tongue was everywhere and when it tired her hands

took over. They stroked, they teased, they gently, very gently raked the taut flesh of his excited organ. Ian looked up and saw her stretching above him. Her hair seemed darker, her body more lithe than before. Her nails seemed blood red in the golden light.

He felt her hand round his testicles. He tried to push himself up. He wanted her more than he'd ever wanted anyone. The blood surged through him. He'd show her what he could do. She was going to get screwed like no-one had ever been screwed before.

Ian felt Angela's hand tighten, her nails biting into the skin of his testicles. He clenched his teeth, it was agony but he didn't want her to stop.

A nail pierced the skin and he yelled out to her to stop. But she didn't. The pain was more than he could stand. He tried to push her off but her nails were tearing at his flesh.

His skin was split, he felt himself being ripped apart. He tried to scream, but her body was smothering him. His balls were being torn from him. There was pain and only pain. And through the pain, he could feel her body, only it was fur not skin against his face.

And her hands seemed to have become claws that were intent on tearing him to little pieces.

Mrs Wert looked in on Ian's bedroom and saw the bed had not been slept in. She wondered where he'd ended up last night. Some girl or other. There seemed to be a different one every evening and it had got worse since the accident. Still there was nothing she could do, so there was no use trying.

Chapter Twelve

Ellen Wert could feel the vomit running down her chin. It was down the front of her dress, too. But she couldn't do anything about it. She was powerless to do anything. She just stood looking at the congealing mess on the Greenes' bed.

It had been 11.30 before she'd managed to get to the Greenes'. She had spent twenty minutes searching for the key, without any luck. It was strange, she'd thought to herself, she could have sworn she'd left it on the hook behind the back door. But it wasn't there. She'd hoped that she hadn't left it in the Greenes' front door.

As it turned out, she hadn't. And that was something. But the only other explanation was that she'd left it inside the Greenes' house. Perhaps in the kitchen, Ellen had thought, when she'd fed the goldfish.

Ellen had been about to go back home when she'd heard a call from two doors down. It had been Mrs Blakey wanting to know if there was anything wrong. Ellen had explained what had happened. Mrs Blakey had sympathized and five minutes later volunteered the information that she had a spare key to the Greenes'. She'd taken in a parcel for them once and forgotten to return the key.

'Would it be any use?' she had asked.

The two women had gone through the front door together. And seen the clothes trailed over the hall and up the stairs, at the same moment. The only difference was that Ellen Wert had recognized them at once. They were Ian's. She had known at once where her key had gone. Her first thought had been to get rid of Mrs Blakey, who had already started to pick up the clothes.

'What's been going on here?' Mrs Blakey had asked. 'Was it like this last time you were here?'

'Perhaps they've come back early,' Ellen had suggested, and knew as she'd said it that she must have sounded daft.

'Someone's broken in and used the place for a party, more likely. I've read about things like that happening in the paper. Just you wait here while I go and fetch my Frank. He'll soon deal with them.' And with that Mrs Blakey had gone off down the Greenes' front path to fetch her husband.

Ellen had called up to Ian, and then, gathering up the clothes as she went, hurried up the stairs to give him a piece of her mind and tell him to get out, double-quick. She'd known from the way the door was shut that they were in the Greenes' bedroom. She'd wondered who it was this time. If it was that Nesbitt girl, she'd have a word or two to say to the girl's mother.

Ellen Wert hadn't bothered to knock. She'd just opened the bedroom door and walked right in. It took her half a minute to take in what she saw. And then she had been violently sick.

She was still being sick when Frank Blakey arrived. But by then she was on her hands and knees beside the bed looking for any part of her son she could recognize.

The news was on the radio and on the television almost immediately the murder was discovered. Frank Blakey had made sure of that, even though the police had told him to keep it to himself. What did they think he was? There was money, real money to be made out of something like this. But you had to move fast.

After the police had finished with him, he'd gone straight back to the house and done a deal with a daily paper, one of the cheap Sundays and the *New Standard*. He'd also got himself an interview on the radio and the television.

But then Frank Blakey was that kind of man. He had always been quick to see an opportunity. And to take advantage of it. Before phoning the newspapers he had arranged with a local wedding photographer to get round to the Greenes' house, quick, and take as many pictures as possible, knowing that by the time the national media arrived there wouldn't be much left to see.

The media, when they did arrive, really went to town on the Wert murder. It was the fourth of its kind and the bloodiest so far. Ian's association with St Michael's was played up big. As too was the fact that all the victims had been at the hospital on the same night some three or four weeks before.

And there was an added mystery this time. A woman with jet-black hair who had been seen leaving the party in Ian Wert's company.

They had also been seen by a neighbour getting out of the car just down from the Greenes', and the police assumption was that the two of them had gone into the Greenes' house.

After that it seemed as if the mystery woman called Angela had just vanished. Police experts had been over the Greenes' house two or three times but had failed to find anything that pointed to the presence in the house of anyone but Ian Wert.

The only fact of any significance that the second detailed examination revealed was the presence of some cat hairs in the Greenes' bedroom.

And the Greenes did not have a cat.

The police appealed for Angela to get in touch with them. And photo-fit pictures appeared on television and in the newspapers. The press linked the mystery woman with the strange presence of cat fur found at the scene of each of the murders, and she was instantly dubbed Cat Woman.

The whole story of Ian Wert's accident and the Wrights'

baby was told over again. A list of other patients' names appeared, including those of Hilary and Roger Wright. The police were inundated with calls from former patients wanting to know if they were in danger, and demanding protection if they were.

For Roger it was a nightmare. He had recognized Ian Wert's name on the news broadcast and then, when he had bought the evening paper, he had seen the van driver's scarred face staring out at him.

Everything about the terrible night came flooding back to him. He could remember every tiny detail now. The conversation in the car with Hilary, even hazy impressions of the journey in the ambulance. And that scream. That terrible, chilling scream that had touched him even while he lay unconscious.

Roger had rung Hilary the minute he'd heard the news of Ian Wert's death, but she wasn't in. He didn't really want to speak to her. Or see her. But he was sure that she had something to do with the killing.

He had bought an early edition of the *New Standard* and read with horror the details of the murder.

But it was the photo-fit picture of the black-haired mystery woman that caught Roger's attention. Was it Hilary? Through Roger's half-closed eyes, it could have been.

His eyes went to the paragraph headed 'Cat Woman', and he felt himself shiver as he read about the traces of cat hair found beside the entrails of Ian Wert's body.

He was sure that the newspaper had more of an eye on circulation than accuracy, but he and Dr Willis knew how near the truth the story was.

According to the police, the murder had been committed late at night. About midnight. Had Hilary been home? Roger couldn't remember. She'd gone out earlier and he had gone to bed before she returned.

Not that he supposed her physical presence was either a

necessary or limiting factor. If he and Dr Willis were right, they were dealing with the supernatural. And that meant anything was possible.

The 'they' or whatever it was that was using Hilary's body – Bast, Dr Willis had called it – might be capable of using other beings too, to do its work.

And what about Ra, the cat? If he could think like a human and in some way transmit his thoughts to Roger when he wanted to, then he must also have supernatural powers at his command.

Roger phoned Hilary again, but there was still no reply. He believed that if he could speak to her he would know whether she had committed the awful murder.

Carol had been with Hilary when she heard about the murder. It was on the television. Carol looked hard at Hilary but she could detect no sign of emotion in her as she sat listening to the grim news. She simply stared straight ahead, stroking Ra all the while with the long tapering fingers of her right hand.

When the news was over, Hilary asked Carol to turn the television off and make them both a cup of coffee.

'How much notice do you have to give?' Hilary asked when they were both settled with their drinks.

'Two weeks, I think. Why?'

Hilary sipped her coffee. She was like a cat herself, Carol thought.

'Because, I think, very soon now, it will be time for you to move in here as we discussed.'

'Has it happened?' Carol asked, wide-eyed and excited.

Hilary shook her head. 'No, but it won't be long.'

'How do you know?' Carol asked.

But she didn't get an answer. Instead Hilary went on to ask her what colour she wanted her room and if there were any special pieces of furniture she wanted to bring with her.

* * *

Roger had been drinking. And by the time he got home the drink and his own fear had pushed his bitterness and his anger with Hilary to new heights. His resentment of Ra, too, and all he stood for was at fever pitch.

There was a picture of Ian Wert on the front page of the *New Standard*. Roger pushed it under Hilary's nose and screamed, 'It was you, wasn't it, you bitch!'

'You're drunk again,' Hilary replied coldly. 'You'd better sleep it off in the spare room. You want to be careful, Roger, you're drinking too much. You'll have another accident one of these nights, or do something silly.'

'You'd like that, wouldn't you?' Roger demanded.

Hilary ignored him and started to get up from the settee. But Roger hadn't finished. He put out an arm and pushed her roughly back on to the sofa.

Hilary fell heavily, disturbing Ra, who was curled up on a cushion. Roger felt the black cat's eyes turn on him like two fierce green searchlights. Ra arched his back and hissed angrily. Hilary put out a hand to comfort him. 'It's all right, darling,' she purred.

'It's not bloody well all right!' Roger shouted and lunged at the cat. 'I'll show the bugger whose house this is.'

Roger never reached Ra. As he moved forward something caught his foot and he took a crashing fall, hitting his head against a small onyx and brass coffee table that stood to one side of the settee.

Roger lay on the carpet. He could feel a trickle of blood running down his cheek. He felt dazed and slightly sick. He opened his eyes. Ra was looking down at him from the arm of the settee. And to Roger it looked for all the world as if the cat's sleek, black, dangerous mouth was twisted into an evil grin.

'I'm going to get rid of that thing', Roger vowed and lost consciousness. When he woke he was on the settee with a plaster on his head. It was 2.30 in the morning and he felt awful.

His head ached and thumped from the drink and the fall. The fall! Roger lifted himself up on one elbow and looked down at the carpet. There was nothing there. Nothing that he could have tripped over. But he knew that he hadn't just fallen, and no matter what Hilary said it hadn't been the drink.

Roger looked up and saw Ra's large, green eyes looking at him. It was the cat that had been responsible for his fall, Roger knew that now. It had been protecting not only itself, but Hilary. And as the knowledge came to Roger so Ra seemed to nod his head in confirmation of the thought. And Hilary confirmed the thought, so that Roger was in no doubt, as the cat turned his back and stalked, slowly and majestically, out of the room. And as he did so a laugh, both wicked and malicious, seemed to fill Roger's head.

The next morning brought more trouble. During the night reporters had been going through the hospital records and talking to staff and patients. The Wrights' name and the unearthly scream on the night of the accident had given rise to stories of a phantom child, so terrible and misshapen, that it had to be put down.

The phone rang three times before 8.30 and each time it was some reporter looking for confirmation of the story. There were newsmen in the street too. And Roger was forced to leave the house via the back gardens of his neighbours' houses.

Hilary remained unconcerned by all the fuss. She refused to answer the phone and, after Roger had left for work, retired to the nursery with Ra and read her book on Egyptian Mythology.

At work, Roger phoned Dr Willis, but there was no reply. It hadn't been difficult to get the number and Roger guessed that, by now, the newspaper men had got it too.

Roger wondered if Dr Willis had gone away or whether he was just not answering the phone. He'd almost called in on his way to work, but in the end he'd decided against it. After all, Dr Willis had made it pretty clear that he didn't want to discuss the matter further at their last meeting. And subsequent events were hardly likely to have changed his mind.

In the middle of the morning, Steve invited him out for a cup of coffee and was a good deal more sympathetic than he'd been for a long while. But then suddenly, Roger noticed, everybody at work was being nice to him. People he hardly knew stopped him and asked him how he and Hilary were coping.

His mother phoned and said that she and his father were thinking about him. And to let them know if there was anything they could do. Although she quickly went on to say that she doubted if there was anything anyone could do under the circumstances.

By mid-afternoon Roger was feeling more hopeful. He had written some copy for the Carter's Cake Company that he was quite pleased with. It was Steve who suggested that maybe it was worthwhile going to the British Museum and doing a spot of research on Bast and any other Egyptian gods of around the same period. And that maybe, while they were at it, they could even look at a couple of books on exorcism, or something like it.

Roger liked the idea, not least because Steve was obviously prepared to come with him. And after the loneliness of the last few weeks, the idea of sharing at least part of the problem with someone else was very welcome.

He had not told Steve everything. Roger had suffered too many laughs and sneers recently to be able to trust anyone completely. One of the things that amazed him was that neither his mother, nor even Steve, who actually worked in a publicity business, could believe him, but they were only too ready to believe the inaccurate, sensationalist theories filling the cheaper newspapers.

Not that Roger was complaining. He was only too grateful to accept whatever support he could get. He arranged with Steve to take an early lunch the next day so that they could go to the British Museum.

Dr Willis had heard about Ian Wert's death on the radio. And later followed the reports on television through the various newscasts. He, probably alone, was neither surprised nor particularly shocked at the murder.

Indeed he had been expecting it. As he now expected his own death. And Roger Wright's. That, he guessed would probably be enough to satisfy the anger of the Egyptian cat-goddess.

Dr Willis pushed himself up from the chair, that he now very rarely left. It was to get himself another drink. A celebration drink. In many ways Ian Wert's death was pleasing. It had proved his theory. And it meant that his own end was not far away. And that was something Dr Willis was increasingly looking forward to.

The days and nights had long since ceased to be separate. Between the drugs and the alcohol he was rarely conscious for any great period of time. He no longer answered the phone, although it had rung a lot since this last murder, and he had told neighbours that he was involved in a series of research experiments and could not be disturbed.

Dr Willis sipped at his drink, his shaking hands knocking the edge of the glass against his teeth, and thought about Roger Wright.

And whether, in his case, death would be enough alone for his crime. In Dr Willis's opinion it would not. Everything he had read recently about ancient Egypt and its gods convinced him that, from Roger, those gods would demand a greater sacrifice, would inflict a crueller punishment, than just the taking of his life.

Hilary was out when Roger got home. There was a note on the kitchen table saying that she would be back about 10 o'clock.

Roger cooked himself a pizza from the deep-freeze, opened a bottle of wine and started to read Hilary's book on Egyptian Mythology.

He became quite absorbed in the stories of the gods and the forms they took. Sometimes the myths contradicted themselves and the gods seemed to be able to change their forms to suit a particular need or occasion.

It was while he was reading about Ra, that Roger became aware of the stillness and the absolute quietness of the house. And it frightened him. He shivered and then jumped at a sudden movement of the door.

'Hilary! Is that you?' he called out.

There was no answer. The door moved again and a black shadow seemed to pass across the doorway. It was a shadow of human proportions. Roger got up from the table and went to the kitchen door and looked out along the hall. There was no-one there.

He saw the door to the lounge move and a minute later Ra appeared. And then Hilary.

'Why didn't you answer when I called?' Roger demanded.

'I didn't hear you,' she replied indignantly. 'Are you all right? You look as white as a sheet.'

'I'm fine. Just tired. I'm going up now,' Roger muttered and went up the stairs to the spare room. When he reached the landing he turned and looked back down the stairs. Hilary was looking up at him, a smile on her face. And in her arms lay Ra, his green eyes staring out of his black face.

Roger turned away. It was then he heard the laughter.

Inside his head. And he knew it was the cat and its mistress mocking him.

Roger lay in the bed in the spare room for a long while before getting to sleep. His head hurt from the fall the previous night. And from his hangover. Through the wall he could hear Hilary talking to the cat.

At one moment she would seem to adopt the tone of voice used to placate a spoilt child. But then it would change, and Roger could hear the huskiness in her voice that reminded him of when they used to make love.

There was laughter too. The laughter of two people who were intimate. Roger hid his head under the bedclothes, under the pillow. But nothing he did could blot out the suspicion of what was going on in the bedroom next door.

It was the cat. If only he could get rid of the cat. Roger was sure Hilary would be all right again. Normal. His old sweet Hilary.

He had read that according to one myth, Ra had to be born as a human and as a cat. The human form was dead. Killed after the accident. Killed in the operating theatre at St Michael's. That's why they were being persecuted. That's why Dr Willis had to die.

Surely if he could kill the cat form then that would be the end of it. Kill the cat! It seemed so simple. Roger wondered why he hadn't thought of it before.

He would go with Steve to the British Museum tomorrow, but he would go with a purpose. Maybe somewhere in all those myths and legends there would be written a way to kill the cat-god once and for all.

Roger turned over on to his other side, suddenly tired and ready for sleep. He closed his eyes, but movement at the window made him open them again. He looked up. The curtains had moved apart at the centre of the window.

The great cat's head seemed to float at the window. The huge green eyes looked down at him. Roger wanted to look away, but he couldn't. He felt himself go cold and shiver, yet there was sweat on his forehead.

He had failed! It was his turn now. Surely he was going to die.

The cat's mouth opened, but there were no words, only laughter. The same, hollow, mocking laughter that Roger had heard before that evening. And Roger knew that it was Ra, or Bast or whoever this thing was, daring him to try and kill it.

Roger got up early the next morning and left the house without seeing Hilary or the cat. There were no newsmen to be avoided, but the papers were still full of Ian Wert's murder and the strange circumstances that surrounded it. There were reports of the mystery woman being seen in a dozen different places around the country. And interviews with at least three women who claimed to be Cat Woman. There was a week-long series in one of the papers under the title 'Hospital of Fear'. It attempted to trace the events from the night of the accident right up to the murder of Ian Wert. There were word portraits of all the victims and Roger noticed that the next article, due to appear the following day, was titled 'Child or Monster?'.

The morning turned out to be busy and he and Steve didn't get away for lunch until 1 o'clock. Roger had not mentioned to Steve his plan to kill Ra. He wanted to, but so much had happened that he no longer really trusted anyone. And anyway, Steve and Sue had a cat of their own and would probably draw the line at helping to plan Ra's death.

The expedition started well enough. There was more reading matter than the two of them could ever have hoped to get through in two years of research, let alone two hours. Stories of Ra abounded: Ra as the Bennu bird, Ra as a falcon, Ra as a lion and as a cat. A cat! The form in which he dismembered Apep.

There were stories of strange deaths, of magical powers and secret rites. But there was nothing that was any use to Roger in his battle with the cat called Ra that now dominated his life.

At 2.30 Steve had to leave to get back to the office. But he urged Roger to stay on, saying he would cover for him. Left alone, Roger decided to go and see some of the antiquities on show in the Egyptian rooms.

Roger found himself increasingly fascinated by the tomb paintings, the religious and secular papyri and the various other objects connected with the burial cult. There were too, the Books of the Dead with their scenes of early Egyptian life and exquisitely carved stone sarcophagi and statues of gods, kings and holy animals.

Roger could almost feel their presence in the artificial stillness of the long, deserted galleries. He wandered on for an hour or more, lost amongst figures of the past. And then, suddenly he was in the Fifth Egyptian room with its small sculptures in gold, silver, bronze and stone. The faces of King Seostius III, Amenophius and the boy-king, Tutankhamun, looked out at him.

But it was the south wall of the room with its display of divine figures that seemed to draw Roger towards it. For there suddenly in front of him was a large bronze, cat-like figure. And without having to read the inscription, Roger knew it to be the incarnation of Bast, the cat-goddess.

Roger stood looking up at the figure. He could feel a strange and potent force flowing out of it. As if it were alive. He felt frightened and began to shake. But still he gazed at the cat-goddess's face. The eyes were alive! And the whole face seemed to come alive. It was the face he'd seen at the window.

For a moment, Roger thought the figure was going to pounce at him, but instead the now grinning mouth opened and hollow, menacing laughter seemed to fill the vast room. Roger turned and fled, taking with him the certain knowledge that he had had his last warning. The next time he heard that awful laugh, there would be no escape.

Chapter Thirteen

Carol Coren hung up her apron, changed her shoes, put on her coat and waited to see the manageress. She was excited. And a little nervous.

Hilary had come in for a cup of coffee earlier, and told her that it was time to give in her notice.

'I know you said it would be soon, but I mean . . . what's happened?' Carol asked.

'Nothing to worry about,' Hilary said, trying to calm her down a little so that the other customers would stop looking at them. 'I made a mistake about the dates, you know how it is?'

'Yes,' Carol agreed, not knowing at all. 'Does Mr Wright know?' she asked.

'You leave Roger to me. He won't be any trouble at all.'

Carol didn't look sure. She'd believed Hilary, all along, but now the time had come to give up her job and her little flat, last minute doubts were beginning to nag her. Hilary put a hand on Carol's arm. 'It will be all right, Carol, I promise you. Remember what I told you, nothing can stop it.'

Hilary had left soon after that and Carol had spent the rest of the morning in a daze. During her own coffee break Carol had gone back over everything that had happened in the last few weeks. Her life had certainly changed since she'd been drawn to Hilary on the night of the accident. And she had to admit it was for the better.

Mind you, any life that didn't have Bill Coren in it had to be an improvement. But there was still a long way to go before her life could be described as comfortable. And the

Wrights' house was a nice one. And the rooms that Hilary had said she would have were miles better than the ones in Waverly Gardens.

Of course it would be all right, Carol told herself. She was being silly. She was looking forward to living with Hilary and looking after Ra, the little one and Roger.

The manageress was very nice when Carol gave in her notice. She said Carol was a hard worker and that if she wanted to go back, at any time, she only had to ask. Carol walked back to her rooms feeling relieved and happy. If, and she was sure it wouldn't, anything went wrong then she had a job to go to. So there was nothing for her to worry about. All she had to do now was to give her landlady, Mrs Nelson, two weeks' notice and everything would be settled.

Carol saw that the off-licence was still open and on the spur of the moment went in and bought a bottle of red wine. Perhaps Hilary would come and have a drink with her. As a sort of celebration. Hilary had told her that they, the Wrights, had wine every evening with their meal and that Carol would be very welcome to join them.

Roger had found it harder to buy the rat poison than he'd thought. He had had to answer a lot of questions about whether he'd informed the local authority and whether there were any young children in the house. And to cap it all the man insisted on taking his name and address and writing it in a small dog-eared notebook.

Roger had made up a name and address on the spur of the moment. Not very convincingly, and as he left the small shop with the tin of poison in his raincoat pocket, he could feel the eyes of the old Indian shopkeeper boring into his back. It was the same on the tube home. He was sure that everyone was looking at him. And certain they knew just what he had in his pocket and what he intended using it for.

The lights were on when Roger got home, and that meant Hilary was home too. Roger transferred the rat poison from his raincoat pocket to his jacket pocket. He would hide it later. In the mean time it seemed safer to keep it with him. After all, he reflected bitterly, it wasn't as if Hilary was likely to throw her arms round him.

As it turned out, Hilary was on her way round to see Carol Coren.

'What about food?' Roger asked.

'Ra and I have eaten,' Hilary said. 'You should have been home in time.'

Roger looked at his watch. It was 7.30. 'We don't usually eat until 8,' he protested.

Hilary shrugged: 'I felt hungry.'

'What time will you be home?'

'I don't know, but don't wait up for me, I probably will be late,' she said and turned and walked down the front path.

Roger went into the lounge, poured himself a large whisky and soda and thought about the plan he'd worked out on the way home. It was a good plan, and Hilary being out for the evening meant that he could make a start on it right away. He finished his drink, double-locked the front door and then made his way down to the garden shed. There he picked up a trowel and a cold hammer and went back to the house, carefully locking the back door behind him. Now, if Hilary should return unexpectedly, he would have plenty of warning.

The cellar was gloomy and damp. The 60 watt light bulb was dangling at the end of a bare wire, moving in the various draughts that squeezed their way between the ill-fitting bricks. Shadows hung suspended in every corner and then jumped suddenly as a fresh gust of wind caught the flex.

Using the trowel and the hammer, Roger worked hard to prise up one of the already cracked flagstones in the corner, by the turn of the stairs. Ten minutes later he was digging in the damp earth beneath the stone. Lovingly he transferred each trowelful of earth to a plastic bag he'd taken from the freezer drawer.

It took about half an hour for Roger to dig a hole deep enough to take the cat's body. When he was satisfied with the grave he put the plastic bag full of earth in the hole and replaced the two halves of the flagstone. Next he pulled an old tea-chest full of unwanted china across the cellar until it sat firmly on the loose flagstone.

Stage one was complete. The grave was ready. All he needed now was to get Hilary out of the house for a day so that he could put the rat poison in Ra's food. Roger picked up his trowel and the hammer, kicked up some dust so that it covered the marks made by the tea-chest and started up the stairs to the house.

The cellar door that he thought he'd shut behind him was open. And standing in the open doorway was Ra. Roger stopped halfway up the stairs and clenched the hammer firmly in his right hand, half expecting to be attacked by the animal. But the cat, after staring at him for a minute longer, merely turned and walked away. And seconds later, Roger heard it go out of the cat-door in the kitchen.

Roger returned the tools to the garden shed, poured himself a very large whisky and took it up to the bathroom with him. There behind the safety of a locked door and cocooned in the warmth of the water he read the instructions on the tin of rat poison.

Later, after he'd got out of the bath and dried himself, Roger prised open the lid of the tin and examined the contents. There was no strong smell to the granules and he felt sure that he could successfully mix enough of the poison into Ra's food, especially if he added in a few of the cat treats that Hilary kept in a silver pillbox in the lounge. Roger put the tin in his dressing gown pocket and cautiously opened the bathroom door. He had not heard Hilary come in, but she moved so quietly these days you could never be sure where she was. And he was particularly anxious to get to bed without seeing her. Hilary had a knack of knowing when he was trying to hide something.

The upstairs landing was empty. Except for Ra who was sitting outside the spare room door. The cat looked at Roger, a long searching look that made him feel nervous. Roger was sure that the cat knew he meant to kill him, and was half expecting some counter-attack. But once again, Ra merely looked and then turned and stalked off down the passage, towards the nursery.

It took another two days before Roger could complete his plan to kill Ra. Two days, during which he so nearly abandoned the idea altogether. When he was at home the cat seemed to follow him everywhere. And if Roger sat down to eat or read a paper or watch television then Ra would sit and watch him.

But there was no communication. No messages as there had been before. And no laughter. Roger felt more and more nervous. He started to make silly mistakes and there were a number of small accidents. And always, when he looked round, there was Ra watching him.

It was Aunt Joan, who unwittingly gave Roger the chance he was waiting for. She rang on Wednesday evening, having just arrived back from a trip to Germany. Hilary was invited over for the day and Roger was asked to join her for a drink in the evening. Roger waited and then let out a sigh of relief as he heard Hilary accept the invitation. It was for Thursday. The next day.

Roger was up early in the morning, before Hilary was awake. He took Ra's bowl and spooned a minimal amount of food into it. Just enough to make it look as if the cat had been fed. Ra quickly ate the little food there was, but Roger left the empty bowl down for Hilary to see.

Next he took Hilary a cup of tea in bed, told her he'd

fed the cat and that he would see her later at her Aunt's. Downstairs, Roger picked up the cat and carried it down to the cellar and put it in a large, empty tea-chest and weighted it down with a small tin trunk. The top was not airtight, but Roger didn't mind that. He just wanted to make sure that he could find the cat when he wanted it.

Roger said goodbye to Hilary and arranged to meet her at Aunt Joan's house at 7 o'clock. The next two hours seemed like two days to Roger. He had phoned Steve and told him that he would be late in. About 12 o'clock, he hoped. They had arranged that Steve would tell anyone who asked, including Hilary, that Roger was in a meeting.

Roger bought a morning paper, looked round a few shops and had two cups of coffee in two different shops. At 10.30 he phoned the house. There was no reply. Roger left it ten minutes and tried again. There was still no answer. Hilary had left for Aunt Joan's. It was time for Roger to return home.

Roger fetched the trowel from the garden shed, barricaded the cat-door and prepared Ra's food before letting the cat out of the cellar. The animal was hungry and made straight for the kitchen and its food bowl. Roger watched as Ra sniffed at the food before finally settling down to eat.

When he was sure the cat was well into his food, Roger went down to the cellar to prepare the grave. He had checked that all the windows were closed and that the door from the kitchen into the hall was shut. It took Roger just ten minutes to move the tea-chest, prise up the loose flagstones and take out the plastic bag full of loose earth. When everything was ready for the burial, Roger went back upstairs and stood at the kitchen door, listening. He could hear the cat crying piteously, but was too frightened to go back into the room and finish the job off.

Instead he went into the lounge and poured himself a large drink. His hands were shaking and he could see in the mirror that his face was white and drawn. Roger sat down in the armchair and tried to calm himself. He told himself it was nearly over, once this was done he was sure everything would be all right. The curse, as he had come to think of it, would be broken.

His glass was empty, Roger looked at his watch. It had been half an hour since he had given the cat the poisoned meal. Reluctantly he got up from the armchair and went back into the kitchen.

He opened the door slowly, cautiously, half expecting the wretched animal to make a dash for it. But he needn't have worried. Ra was by the back door, his long, slim black body twisted into an ugly shape.

The animal had been sick. And there were deep claw marks on the back door to the garden. Roger got a bucket of water and some Flash and the kitchen mop and started to clear up the mess. The cat hadn't moved, but Roger could feel its eyes following him wherever he went. When he had cleaned up the sick, Roger moved cautiously towards the dead body and began to pick it up.

But Ra wasn't dead. Not quite. The black cat hissed and spat, lashing out at Roger with an angry claw. Roger felt his flesh tear and saw blood spurt from the back of his left hand. He threw the cat to the floor and heard it screech with pain as it hit the hardness of the tiles.

Roger went over to the sink, turned on the tap and held his bleeding hand under the cold water. The wound looked clean enough, but Roger made a mental note to put some Dettol on it later. He felt something pluck at his trouser leg and looked down. Ra had dragged himself across the kitchen and was now desperately clawing his way up Roger's trouser leg. Roger shook his leg violently, but the cat hung on grimly.

There was a heavy frying pan on the draining board. Roger picked it up in his right hand and struck at the cat's head. He struck again. And again in a blind fury at the cat that had wrecked his life.

The small, black body fell to the floor and lay quite still in a pool of blood. Roger picked it up and carried it quickly down to the cellar. The cat fitted easily into the grave and by pressing the earth down hard on top of the body, Roger was able to fit in all the earth from the plastic bag. Next, he pushed the broken flagstone back into place, before finally stirring up the dust from the cellar floor so that when it settled it would cover every trace of his activity.

Roger gave a grim smile of satisfaction as he looked down at his handiwork. It was almost impossible to tell, in the dim light, that the floor had been disturbed. Before going upstairs to clean up he moved the tea-chest back over the grave.

It took Roger half an hour to clean up the kitchen. And himself. He was just about to leave the house when the front doorbell rang. Roger ducked back into the kitchen and hoped that whoever it was hadn't seen his shadow through the glass. The bell rang again. Roger stayed where he was.

Outside on the front doorstep, Carol Coren was puzzled. She was sure there was someone in. She'd heard noises. And when she rang the bell she could have sworn that she'd seen a shape or shadow disappear into the kitchen. She was also sure that it was not Hilary who was inside the house. Perhaps Mr Wright was home, but if he was, why didn't he answer the door? She rang the bell again and looked at her watch.

She'd have to go back in a minute. Mrs Wilkinson had only given her permission to slip out for ten minutes so she could have another look at her new room and work out what to do with some of her belongings. But she couldn't be all day.

Carol bent down and looked through the letter-box.

Everything looked normal. Perhaps she'd been mistaken. Anyway she couldn't wait any longer. She straightened up, picked up her bag and went back down the front path.

Roger waited another ten minutes after he heard the letter-box flap clank back into place before poking his head round the side of the kitchen door. There was nothing on the mat. And no-one on the doorstep. Whoever it was had given up and gone away. Roger picked up his briefcase and left the house as unobtrusively as possible.

From early in the morning, Dr Willis had known that today was the day. And as if to make it easier for the enemy he had opened the curtains and a window in the kitchen for the first time in weeks. He felt quite calm about dying, but he had to admit that this was probably due to alcohol and the drugs he was still pumping into his emaciated frame.

Dr Willis smiled to himself as he remembered how the victims had died. They won't get much of a meal out of me, he thought. He gave himself a last injection and put a fresh bottle of whisky on the little table by his chair. And waited.

It was the black cat that came. The one that had watched him from the very beginning. It just simply landed on his lap during one of the many periods of semi-consciousness that he had started to experience over the last few days.

Dr Willis looked at the animal through half-open eyes. The animal stared back at him. And then, without warning, stretched out a paw and clawed out the doctor's right eye. Dr Willis had time to feel the searing pain before the animal ripped off his left ear and opened a gash in his cheek that exposed the bone.

The cat paused and licked its bloodied paw and studied the mess it had made of Dr Willis's face. Dr Willis was making small whimpering noises. But the cat soon stopped that. His paw flicked out again, this time hooking its razor-sharp claws into Dr Willis's tongue. When it was quite sure the claws were firmly rooted in the soft pink flesh, the cat started to pull. Dr Willis's head jerked forward, but the cat placed his other paw against the doctor's forehead and continued to pull, relentlessly shredding the tongue until it hung flapping from the old man's mouth.

It took the cat fifteen minutes to reduce Dr Willis's head to a carcass, picked clean of every scrap of flesh.

Roger never made Aunt Joan's for drinks. He had gone out for a celebration drink with Steve at lunchtime, not that Steve knew they were celebrating. And Roger, at least, had gone on celebrating at 5.30 with practically anyone he could find.

The celebration went on long and loud. It went from pub to pub and then on to a restaurant and on again to a club. It was very late when Roger got home. But Hilary was still up, waiting for Ra. She asked Roger if he'd seen the cat, but Roger wasn't in a state to answer any question sensibly. Hilary gave up the struggle, she didn't ask him any more questions, not even where he'd been or why he hadn't met up with her at Aunt Joan's house.

Roger was grateful. He climbed unsteadily up the stairs, threw off his clothes and went into the bathroom. His hand hurt where Ra had scratched him. He took off the plaster Barbara at work had got for him, and examined the wound. It had turned septic and a yellowish pus was oozing from one end of the scratch.

Roger washed the hand in warm water and then dabbed Dettol along the length of the wound. He wondered if Hilary had noticed the plaster. If she had, he was going to say he'd cut it on an art knife at work, while helping Steve mount a layout.

Roger opened the door of the bathroom and stopped dead. He blinked his eyes, unwilling to believe what he saw. Along the hall, sitting outside the spare room door, was Ra. Roger felt his legs go weak. It couldn't be. The cat was dead. And buried, two feet deep in the cellar.

'Hilary!' Roger screamed. 'Hilary, come here.'

Hilary came up the stairs fast in response to Roger's call. But she didn't look very pleased about it.

'What is it?' she asked. 'You look awful.'

'I thought you were looking for the bloody cat,' Roger said.

'Yes.'

'Well, there it is. Sodding thing,' Roger replied, pointing to the spare room door.

'Where?'

Roger looked again. There was no sign of the cat. 'Well, he was there, a minute ago.'

'If this is one of your jokes, Roger, I don't think it's very funny,' Hilary said. 'I'm worried about him.'

Roger went into the spare room and started calling the cat. Hilary followed him. There was no sign of Ra. At Roger's insistence they searched the whole of the top of the house. But there was still no sign of Ra.

'I'm going back downstairs,' Hilary said, icily. 'You're so drunk it's a wonder you're not seeing pink elephants. If I were you I'd get to bed and sleep it off.'

Roger got into bed and switched off the bedside light. He felt cold and shivery despite the thick double duvet that covered him. He closed his eyes and immediately found himself re-living the scene in the kitchen that morning. He started to sweat. It must be guilt, Roger thought. Perhaps it was how murderers felt. Roger had never killed anything before.

'Yes you have.'

The voice seemed to fill Roger's head. He sat up in bed

and switched on the light. He was on his own. There was no-one in the room. The door was still closed. 'You have killed twice, now,' the voice whispered. 'You and the others. You have killed Ra, son of Bast, Ruler of upper and lower Egypt and all the worlds above the skies and below the waters. The other five have been punished. There is only you left. And soon you will be called to pay your debt. Then Ra can be born again, of woman, and in his own kingdom.'

The voice stopped. Roger sat absolutely still. It was as if some huge, invisible hand was holding him against the brass bedhead.

So it hadn't ended. Killing Ra had achieved nothing. The thing could not be stopped. The voice had said that the other five had been punished, so by now, Roger guessed, Dr Willis must be dead too. Roger realized that he hadn't seen a newspaper or heard a news broadcast since the morning.

His shoulders slumped forward, as if the invisible force had suddenly released him, tears started to run down his cheeks. He'd thought he'd won. But now he knew that only the thing, Bast, Ra, whatever it was called, could win. He slid down under the duvet and sobbed into his pillow. It was a long time before he got to sleep.

It was a long time before Hilary got to sleep, too. And it wasn't just Ra's absence that she was thinking about. It was something that Aunt Joan had told her that kept her awake.

Hilary had told her aunt about Carol, and asked her if she'd ever met Carol's family when she'd lived in the village.

Her aunt's face had clouded and it had taken Hilary a good half an hour to get her to explain.

Hilary had been shocked by the explanation, but not for the reason her aunt had expected. Perhaps shocked wasn't the right word, anyway. Amazed might be more accurate.

Yes, that was it, Hilary thought, she was amazed at the way in which events, life for her and Ra, and Roger, were being ordered.

Chapter Fourteen

The weekend news media really went to town on Dr Willis's death. There were interviews with the police, psychiatrists, priests, and ghost-hunters, as well as with the relatives of the five murder victims.

Headlines ranged from 'Angel of Death claims fifth victim!' to 'Fifth Ripper Victim'. The whole story of the road accident, together with more invented details of the birth and death of the Wright child, appeared in at least two Sunday papers. Ian Wert's mother had written about her son in another paper, and there were photographs of everyone connected with the deaths.

At least three patients, one seriously ill, had discharged themselves from St Michael's saying they were too frightened to stay. Several of the hospital staff had stayed away from evening shifts and more had asked for a transfer to other hospitals.

The Wrights' house had become an object of curiosity and neither Roger nor Hilary felt like going out and braving the stares and comments of sightseers, or the increasingly suspicious and even hostile glances of neighbours.

For two days the two of them led their own separate existence in the same house. Hilary had not mentioned Roger's drunkenness, but she had asked him if he'd come home during the day on Friday when Ra had disappeared.

She had also asked if he'd noticed the deep claw mark on the back door. Roger had answered no to both questions.

Hilary did not seem unduly worried by Ra's disappearance. It was as if she knew that he would come back when he was ready.

Roger wondered if the voice had spoken to her. Or, for

one moment, if Hilary was the voice. At other times he wondered if he'd even heard the voice at all. Perhaps it was all in his imagination. But he knew it was not. He had killed the cat. And five people had died. Ugly, violent deaths that could only be explained by the presence of a force that was beyond human knowledge and understanding.

The weekend passed slowly. And Roger grew more and more restless. He wanted to go down to the cellar and check that Ra's grave was undisturbed, but he didn't dare with Hilary in the house.

He was worried also about the wound on the back of his hand. It was not healing. It ached and throbbed and towards the end of Sunday, it started to itch badly.

Roger went to bed on Sunday night, but he couldn't sleep. Every time he closed his eyes he saw the dead cat's body. Sometimes it was the scene in the kitchen, at other times it was as if the animal were still alive and was there, sitting looking at him.

That's how it was on Sunday night. And once, just as he thought he might drop off, Roger could have sworn that something jumped on to the bed.

At 2 A.M. Roger was still awake. He switched on the bedside lamp and got quietly out of bed. He put on his dressing gown and tip-toed out into the passage. Everything was quiet. He moved silently, lightly down the passage and stopped outside Hilary's door. There was no sound.

Roger went on, down the stairs and along the hall to the cellar door. He paused and listened again before opening it, but he could hear nothing.

He closed the cellar door behind him, before turning on the light. It seemed dingier than ever. Roger picked his way slowly and carefully down the stone steps and turned to face the place where he'd buried Ra. It was exactly as he'd left it.

Except for just one thing. Heading away from the tea-chest was a set of paw marks clearly imprinted in the dust. They led towards the outside wall of the house. And stopped abruptly.

Roger stood and looked at the paw marks for a long time. He didn't have to move the tea-chest or the flagstones to know what the marks meant. The cat was free.

Roger did not know where it was, but he did know that somewhere, in one world or another, Ra was waiting for him. And that their last meeting was not far away.

Roger went back upstairs to the kitchen and made himself a cup of tea. Like Dr Willis, he felt strangely calm. His mind was brilliantly clear, all uncertainty had gone.

He didn't understand what was happening or how it was happening, but Roger was clear about the need for him to accept whatever punishment the cat-goddess ordained.

Judith Wright had read and heard about Ian Wert's and Dr Willis's deaths with an increasing feeling of unease.

She knew that all her worst fears, that night in the hospital, were about to be realized. And that there was nothing she could do. It made her feel guilty. Especially in view of her new-found happiness with Lionel.

It seemed wrong, somehow, to be enjoying life so much when Roger was so lost. And especially wrong that the enjoyment was of such a basic kind.

Judith felt herself getting excited and looked at her watch. Lionel wouldn't be home for another two hours. And then they would have to be quick if he was going to get anything to eat for his lunch.

Perhaps she'd go and get changed in a minute, then she'd be ready for him when he got home. Judith looked at herself in the mirror, she couldn't believe how she'd changed. She was awful. She'd never been like this before. She wanted it all the time now. And the things they did. Mind you, Lionel was just as bad. And him in his fifties.

What had happened to them? Judith didn't like to admit it, but she knew that somehow it was all connected with Roger's accident. That was why she felt guilty. She decided to ring Roger at work and see how he was.

Hilary had been quite unprepared for the phone call from Roger's boss and the suggestion that he pop round and have a word or two with her. But she had agreed and now as she waited for him to arrive, she wondered, not for the first time, why Robin Edwards wanted to talk to her about Roger. And without 'saying anything to your husband' as he'd put it.

But then, of course, they didn't know that Roger wouldn't be with the agency much longer. Hilary doubted if Roger had told them. She also doubted whether Roger yet realized the full extent of the plans they had for him. Certainly the two of them had never talked about it. But Hilary was pretty sure that Bast, with all her power, had let Roger know that things were about to change for him.

The doorbell rang. Hilary patted her hair, removed an imaginary speck of dust from her dress and went to open the door. Robin Edwards was the Creative Director of the agency where Roger worked. And he believed in looking very creative. Hilary had met him before at the odd office party, but even she was taken aback by the figure that shook her hand and followed her into the lounge.

'Do you like it?' he asked Hilary, who had been staring at his outfit in pale green and salmon pink. 'I had it run up for me by Tommy . . . Nutter, you know.'

'It's very nice, Robin,' Hilary said. 'Would you like a drink or a cup of coffee?'

'Have you any China tea?'

'Yes.'

'A cup of that, please. Perhaps I could make it. It's such an individual taste, you know.'

Hilary showed Robin into the kitchen and sat at the

scrubbed, pine table while he made himself a pot of China tea.

'There,' he said, ten minutes later, during which time he had managed to transfer vast quantities of boiling water from kettle to teapot, to sink and then start all over again, before finally pouring himself a cup of the amber liquid.

'Shall we go back into the lounge?' Hilary offered.

'No, let's stay here. It's so much nicer in the kitchen. You know, I've been thinking about having my office done out as a kitchen, we've so many food and drink accounts at the agency. And then, of course, there's all our retail business. Yes, I shall definitely think about it. Now, Hilary, let's get on with what I've come to talk about.'

'Yes.' Hilary nodded.

'It's Roger,' Robin said, and then sipped his tea for fully a minute.

'Roger?' Hilary prompted.

'Now, we all know what a hard time he, well both of you, have had. And I think I can say that we, and particularly me, have done our best to be sympathetic. I mean there was the car. And, of course, he has had a lot of time off.'

'You've all been very good, to both of us,' Hilary agreed, quickly. Robin smiled, graciously and half waved a hand, before going on.

'Well, as I was saying, we've all been very sympathetic. And, of course, we still are, but my colleagues and I would like to think that his, your troubles will soon be over. And that Roger can get back to, well, full power, shall we say.' There was a long pause while Robin sipped his tea.

'Has Roger spoken to you recently?' Hilary asked.

'What about, dear?'

Hilary gave a little shrug. 'Anything, his problems, the accident?'

Robin shook his slightly thinning blonde hair. 'No. To be honest we haven't seen too much of Roger recently. And, of course, there are so many demands on my time. Why?'

'Well, I know you've all been very kind, and patient, but between you and me, Robin, Roger is not well. The accident and all the publicity has been too much for him. He blames himself, terribly, for the death of the baby. I don't know whether you know, but we, I can't have any more children . . .'

Robin said he didn't know and that he was very sorry.

'Well,' Hilary went on, 'I think, we think, everything that's happened, those ghastly deaths at the hospital, have affected Roger's mind. He's started to believe some of those stories in the newspapers. And now, he blames me and the baby for the death of all those people.'

Hilary looked sad. Robin lent forward and patted her hand. Hilary waited a moment before going on. And then, very quietly as if it required great courage, she said, 'We think it would be better if Roger went away somewhere, right away from everything that's happened. Somewhere where he can get some peace and quiet. Perhaps then he'll be able to sort the whole thing out in his mind, and come to terms with it.'

Robin lent forward across the table until his face was only a few inches away from Hilary. She remembered now that he had this habit of moving close to people when he got intense.

'Are you saying, Hilary, that Roger is going to have to leave the agency?' Robin demanded.

'I think, we think, it would be for the best, Robin. As you say, you've all been very kind to him, but he needs time now. Perhaps when it's all over . . . well, perhaps he can come and see you all . . .'

'Yes. Yes, of course, my dear,' Robin said expansively. 'If there is anything we can do, you know we will.'

'There is one thing . . .'
'Ask.'
'I'd rather Roger told you about leaving, himself. So could you not do or say anything until he comes to see you. It won't be long, I promise. You do understand, don't you . . .?'
Robin did understand. And although he didn't say so was very satisfied with the way his little chat had turned out. Roger was, well, had been very good, in his own way, but there was no shortage of good people, not with so many out of work. And really it had all turned out to be rather nasty. Those awful deaths and everything. And, of course, the advertising business was so sensitive.
And there was that young writer he'd seen only a few weeks ago. Robin had been very taken with the look of his work. So perhaps, all in all, everything was working out for the best.
It was left that Robin would wait for Roger to come and see him. And that, in the mean time, if there was anything that Robin or the agency could do, Hilary had only to ask.

Judith Wright was changing her clothes and getting more excited by the minute. The telephone conversation with Roger had not been easy. They had very little to say to each other. And Roger had sounded most peculiar, which hadn't made things easier. Judith wondered if he was on drugs, his mood seemed to change so abruptly. At the end of five minutes there had been a long silence, followed by a hasty goodbye from Roger, and that had been the end of their conversation.
Judith shrugged impatiently at the thought of Roger and his problems and finished dressing. She hoped Lionel would be home on time. She didn't think she could wait much longer.
Their games took up practically all her time now. She spent her time either getting ready, or making a new

costume for one or the other of them, for the new fantasies they acted out. Judith was amazed at how real the games had become. And how good they had both got at acting. Lionel made a wonderful woman. And she had to admit as she looked in the mirror that she made a very convincing German officer.

Roger looked down at his hand. The one that Ra had scratched. The wound had dried up, but now there was something else. Roger had noticed it when he was talking to his mother on the phone.

There was a line of silky, black hair growing along the line of the scratch.

He was sure that it hadn't been there when he'd left home that morning. And he didn't think it had been there when he was typing that television script for the Miller's beans commercial, just half an hour ago.

Roger put the hand away in his pocket, and tried to think about work. Five minutes later he took the hand out of his pocket and looked at it again.

Was it his imagination, or had the band of hair got just a bit wider. And a bit longer?

Roger couldn't be sure.

He picked up a ruler and measured the line of silky, black hair. It was just over 3 centimetres long and half a centimetre wide.

Steve walked into the office just as Roger was taking the ruler away from his hand.

'What are you doing?' Steve asked with a laugh.

'Measuring the scratch that bloody cat inflicted on me.'

'How is it?' Steve asked.

'Fine,' Roger said abruptly and hid his hand below the desk.

Robin Edwards felt uneasy. The more he thought about it, the more strange he found his little chat with Hilary.

Now he thought about it, there had been a strange atmosphere in the house. He had felt it the moment he had entered the front door. He was sensitive to atmosphere. And he just knew that something in the house was not quite right.

It wasn't so much what Hilary had said, although the way she kept saying 'I' and then changing it to 'we' was definitely odd, but something about the way in which she had spoken the words. It was as if she were playing a game. Almost as if she were waiting for him to react before she moved on to the next bit of the story.

Almost, Robin thought, as if she were making the story up as she went along.

And then, perhaps there was the strangest thing of all, the laughter.

It was immediately after Robin had left the house, while he was still on the doorstep. It had raised the hair on the back of his neck. A long, cruel laugh that seemed to escape from the house and echo round his head. And then, it was as if another voice had joined in, sharing the joke, so to speak, at the expense of a third person.

And somehow, Robin knew that the third person was Roger Wright.

Robin wondered if he should speak to Roger. But he didn't know what to say. It all sounded so silly when he thought about it. He was letting his imagination run away with him. All that stuff on the television and in the newspapers. Christ, he'd end up like Roger if he didn't watch it. He would let events take their course. It would be better all round if Roger left the agency. At least that way, Robin Edwards would be in the clear, if something unfortunate happened. And so too, would the agency.

Several times during the day, Roger measured the band of silky, black hair on the back of his hand, to see if it had got any bigger. But it had not. And by the time the late afternoon had come he felt much more relaxed about it. On the train home behind the anonymity of the evening paper Roger asked himself just what he'd been so worried about.

Had he really thought he was turning into some kind of animal? He laughed out loud, forgetting where he was. And felt rather foolish when he saw several people turn and look at him. He went back to the paper, counting off the stations automatically as he read.

There were two more stops to go when he put the paper down and became aware of a young woman in a large red hat staring at him from across the gangway.

Roger followed her eyes down and he knew that she was looking at his hand.

He forced himself to look down too.

Christ!

He put the hand in his pocket. He could feel himself shaking. The train came to a stop. It wasn't Roger's station but he got out all the same.

What was happening to him? The silky, black hair had spread. The patch was longer, nearly over the knuckle. And wider too, at least twice the width it had been when he left the office. He kept his hand in his pocket, not daring to look at it again until he was on his own.

There was a telephone box on the corner by the chemist. Roger opened the door and went inside. The phone was broken, but he didn't mind. He took his hand out of his pocket and examined it, reluctantly. The patch was bigger. Not a lot. But definitely bigger than it had been on the train.

He felt the shaking start again. He needed a drink. A large drink. But what was he going to do about the hand? He couldn't keep it in his pocket the whole time. Roger saw the sign above the chemist's shop. There must be something at the chemist's that would cover up the patch of silky, black hair.

Roger made himself calm down. When he had stopped shaking he walked slowly out of the telephone box, across the pavement and into the chemist.

The shop was empty. A large woman came through from a doorway behind the counter and asked if she could help. Roger kept his hand in his pocket and asked for a packet of lint and a roll of sticky plaster.

'What size lint?' the woman asked. 'Is it for your hand?' she went on, looking at the rather strange way Roger was holding his arm.

'No!' Roger almost shouted. 'It's not. It's not for me at all. It's for someone else. Um, a medium size will do, thank you.'

The woman looked at him suspiciously. Roger was sure she was about to call the police. If only she'd just give him the lint and the sticky plaster, he could get out of the place.

The bell on the door behind him jangled and a young couple came in. The woman put the lint and the plaster in a bag and handed it across the counter to Roger.

'That'll be £1.23,' she said.

Roger took the bag with his good hand and put it in his pocket. Then he reached across the front of his body and put the right hand in his left trouser pocket, where he kept his money. He took out £2 and handed it to the woman.

He thought she was going to say something but the young couple were waiting and in the end she just handed him his change. Roger muttered a quiet thank you and made a grateful escape.

He turned left out of the shop and walked several hundred yards down a dark side road, before stopping to take the plaster and the lint out of the chemist's bag. Scissors! He'd meant to buy some scissors to cut the lint and the plaster. He opened the packet of lint and by using his teeth and hands managed to tear off a piece, roughly the size of the patch of hair.

Roger placed the lint over the hair and started to bind it to his hand with the sticky tape. It was difficult using just his right hand, but eventually the pad of lint and the hair was completely covered.

Roger had three large whiskies in quick succession at the Cross Keys, a dingy pub just round the corner from the tube station. He would look at his hand in the morning, he decided, and if it was worse he would go and see the doctor. There was probably a very simple explanation. Roger remembered hearing how people had lost their hair overnight. And about others, who just as inexplicably, had started growing hair after years of baldness.

It probably had nothing to do with Ra at all. Or, if it had, it was a simple allergy that could be cleared up with a few pills or some ointment.

Much to his surprise, Roger found that Hilary had waited dinner for him. She seemed in a good mood and they chatted away to each other, about this and that, for most of the evening. At 10 o'clock Hilary said she was going to bed. She kissed Roger on the forehead and ran her hand through his hair. It was a pleasant sensation. And Roger wished she'd do it again.

After Hilary had gone upstairs, Roger felt restless. His hand, under the lint and the sticking plaster, was itching. Roger prowled around the house, going from one room to another, without being able to settle anywhere.

He went into the kitchen and stood by the back door. It was a nice night. He opened the door and went out into the garden. Roger took a deep breath. There was a gentle breeze blowing that seemed to carry on it a dozen different and tantalizing smells that he had never been aware of before. He walked round the garden and was amazed at the number of new sensations that assailed his senses.

The garden looked different too. Roger was seeing it

through new eyes. The movement of leaves across the grass, the passage of a bird, the intriguing rustle of a bush. All were new to him. And totally absorbing.

A strong gust of wind brought with it a new smell, a scent, a flavour that made Roger instantly hungry.

It was coming from the direction of the Potters, just three doors down, along to the left. Roger opened the side gate and strolled out on to the pavement. Even the street looked different tonight. Roger couldn't explain it, but he knew it was something to do with the other changes that he sensed were taking place in him. He was sharper, more alert. Everything seemed more real than usual, more immediate.

He kept close to the fence and the front wall of the Fergusons' garden, working his way along slowly until he came to the Potters.

Roger paused at the Potters' gate and turned his head, gently sniffing the night air as he did so. The smell, the delicious smell was definitely coming from the Potters' garden. Roger opened the gate an inch or two and squeezed his way into the front garden.

The house was in darkness. The Potters must have gone to bed. Roger moved up the paved, side pathway. The smell was growing stronger. And with each step, Roger's hunger grew too. He had to taste whatever was making that delicious . . . fish, that was it, that fishy smell!

And it was coming from the dustbin just in front of him. The dustbin! Roger didn't know what he'd expected, but suddenly he felt a deep sense of disappointment. He turned to go. Or, at least, that's what he meant to do. But instead he found himself lifting the lid off the Potters' dustbin.

He couldn't help himself. He had to have that delicious fishy smell for himself. His right hand dipped into the dustbin and raked around the Potters' rubbish. The wind blew again, hard, dislodging the dustbin lid. It fell with a clatter on the path. The noise was deafening.

Roger stood perfectly still. His body tense, ready to make a run for it if Arthur Potter came to investigate the noise. But he didn't. Slowly, Roger let himself relax.

The smell was still there, but he was frightened to go back to the dustbin. He waited on the side path a moment longer. He was ashamed of himself. What was he doing going through the Potters' dustbin? What on earth was happening to him?

He heard a car cruising along the street and hung back in the shadow of the house. It was a Panda car. It slowed as it passed the Potters' gate and then disappeared on up the road.

Roger waited until he was sure it had gone and then made a dash for home. Back in the warmth of the kitchen, he felt safer. But he was still hungry. He could still smell that smell. He sniffed at his sleeve. Yes, it was there: he must have brushed against the tin with his coat.

Roger looked round the kitchen. There was another smell coming from somewhere and it was almost as tempting as the one in the Potters' dustbin.

His eye rested on Ra's bowl. Of course. Every night since he'd disappeared, Hilary had religiously filled the cat's silver bowl with fresh food ready for the animal's return.

Roger went over to the bowl. It was full of plump, meaty pilchards. His hand moved towards the bowl. There was nothing he could do to stop it. Roger stooped down and picked up the bowl and carried it over to the kitchen table. He knew what he was doing. What he had to do. Even though he hated the thought of it. And hated himself for doing it.

His head moved towards the bowl. He tried to stop it, but he was powerless. It was as if some unseen force was pressing his head and shoulders down into the bowl. There was no fighting it. And deep down, Roger knew that part of him didn't want to fight it. Part of him wanted, more than anything else, that delicious smelling fish.

Chapter Fifteen

Carol Coren sat alone, cuddled up in the big armchair, in her room. She had finished packing the few possessions she had to take with her to Hilary's house. Now there was nothing to do until the next evening when she was due to move in. It seemed a strange time to move, but then Carol had given up trying to understand everything that Hilary decreed. She just accepted that if Hilary said it had to be this way, or that way, then that was how it had to be.

Carol was excited. She wondered what life would be like with the Wrights. And how the five of them would fit in together.

It was Mr Wright, Roger, that she was unsure about. She didn't really know him at all. Mind you, he was very handsome. Carol closed her eyes and imagined looking after him. That was what Hilary had said she would have to do. Although she hadn't said why.

'Poor Roger,' Carol thought, perhaps he had some awful disease that was gradually getting worse. Perhaps she would end up having to do everything for him. Carol found the idea exciting. She hadn't really thought about men in that way since she'd left Bill.

But the idea of undressing Roger, and doing things to his body was making her very excited. Carol got up from the armchair and took off her clothes. She took them off very slowly, in front of the mirror, imagining all the time that it was Roger Wright rather than her own reflection that watched her.

When she was naked, she lay on the bed and ran her hands over her body. She imagined they were Roger's . . .

why did she want to say, hand, not hands? Carol closed her eyes, tightly and tried to imagine herself making love with Roger. Her hands moved lower, until they were between her legs. She was wet, very wet. She started to move slowly up and down, rubbing herself against the hardness of her fist.

She could almost hear Roger crying out. He was asking for help. She could see his face. And suddenly the rest of his body. His body! What was wrong with his body? It was . . . poor Roger!

Now she understood! Of course, she would help him. Carol moved so that she was kneeling, legs astride, on the bed. She wanted to help Roger so badly. She looked round frantically for something hard, anything that would take Roger's place until she could be with him.

Her hairbrush. It was on the bedside table. She reached over and picked it up. She put it to her lips and kissed it tenderly, before letting it travel down the front of her body. When it lay on the bed between her legs, she lowered herself on to it, whispering Roger's name, over and over again.

It was late when Roger woke. Too late, he decided, to go to work. He lay in bed listening to the noises that filtered through the window and the bedroom door. It was as if he was hearing them for the first time, with a different kind of ear.

Hilary didn't come in to see him. And a little later he heard the front door close behind her. He wondered where she was off to now.

Roger waited five minutes and then got up. He went over and stood in front of the long mirror set in the door of the wardrobe and stripped off his pyjamas.

Fine, silky, black hair had started to cover his body. In parts it was quite thick. Roger looked down at his hand, the one Ra had scratched, and ripped off the plaster. The hair was thicker than it had been the night before when he'd put the plaster on.

Roger felt sick. He made his way over to the bed and sat on the edge of it, his head in his hands. He knew what was happening to him. But he didn't want to admit it. And he didn't want to think about where it would stop.

Roger thought of the others who'd died such horrible deaths and for a minute wished that he could have shared their punishment. However terrible it had been.

He knew now that Dr Willis had been right, some very special punishment had been reserved for him.

Roger went into the bathroom and took out his electric razor. There was a gadget on the back for trimming long hair on his face and neck. He switched the shaver on and applied it to the back of his hand. The teeth of the comb dragged and pulled at the fine, black hair. Little rivers of blood appeared where the teeth bit into his flesh, but slowly the black fur began to disappear.

Half an hour later, Roger was ready to go out. His hand was sore, but at least it looked relatively normal. He had no idea where he was going when he left the house, he just knew he wanted to be out when Hilary returned.

Robin Edwards put the phone down and sat very still and very quiet for a long while. He had been speaking to Hilary Wright.

'You look funny, are you all right?' Sarah, his P.A., asked.

'I'm not quite sure.'

'Do you want anything? A cup of coffee or something?'

'Well, perhaps something a little stronger. A brandy, I think.'

Sarah Francis went over to the white cocktail cabinet in the corner of the office and poured her boss a large brandy. 'What on earth did she say to make you so upset?' Sarah asked.

Robin gulped at the brandy. 'It wasn't really what she

said . . . although it seems very funny that Roger didn't ring himself . . . it was the way she said it.'

'But what did she say?' Sarah insisted.

'She said Roger wouldn't be coming back to work again.'

Sarah shrugged, she wasn't really very surprised. There had been lots of stories going round the agency about Roger. A lot of people thought that the accident and the loss of the baby had sent him dotty.

It was a pity, Sarah thought, he was good-looking, and nice. She quite fancied him.

'Shall I start a collection for him?' she asked Robin. 'We could send the present on.'

'Yes, that would be nice,' Robin agreed. 'Here you are, I'll start it off,' he said and handed her a five pound note. 'And perhaps we could do a card, as well.'

'Where's he going?' Sarah asked.

'Away. But I'm not sure where.'

Hilary was glad Roger had gone out. The builder was coming at 12 o'clock and it would be much easier with Roger out of the way. The changes she wanted to put in hand would make life easier for all of them. But she didn't expect Roger to understand that. Not just yet.

The change she had in mind meant that Roger wouldn't have to use the stairs. And during the day, Carol could be near him while she got on with the rest of her duties.

Although in view of what her aunt had told her she realized that all of their relationships would change now. Perhaps duties was no longer the right word.

Steve had tried phoning Roger the minute he'd heard the news, but there was no reply. The story had gone round the agency like wildfire. Not that it was much of a story to begin with, but then people had started adding bits until no-one knew what to believe.

Steve had also phoned Sue, but she too seemed to be out. Why hadn't Roger told him, yesterday? It seemed so strange to suddenly go and quit like that. And why had Hilary rung Robin? Why hadn't Roger come in, or at least, rung up himself?

The phone rang. Steve answered it: 'Steve Palmer.'

'Steve, it's Roger.'

'Roger, where are you?'

'Look, I'm not coming in today, I wondered if we could meet for a drink?'

'I know you're not coming in today. The whole agency knows you've quit. Why didn't you say something yesterday?'

There was silence at the other end of the phone.

'Roger? Are you still there?'

'Steve, what do you mean, I've quit?' Roger asked quietly.

Steve Palmer held the receiver more tightly in his hand. He realized his palm was greasy with perspiration.

'Are you saying you haven't left the agency?' Steve asked.

'Why do you think I have?' Roger continued suspiciously.

'Because Hilary phoned up Robin this morning and said you wouldn't be coming in again. Look, Roger, what's going on?'

There was a silence. And then Roger said, 'I don't know, Steve. I don't know.'

They arranged to meet for a drink, at 1 o'clock, in the Talisman, a quiet pub in one of the squares behind the office.

No-one from the agency used it, so they would be on their own. Roger was already there when Steve arrived. He looked strained and tired. And a little unkempt. It was as if he hadn't shaved for a couple of days, Steve thought.

Steve ordered himself a pint of bitter and Roger a large

scotch. When the drinks arrived, Roger suggested they go over to the corner farthest from the door. It was dark.

They sipped their drinks and looked slightly embarrassed at each other, neither of them knowing where to start.

Steve noticed that Roger's hands were shaking. 'You all right?' he asked.

Roger nodded. 'Tell me about me leaving,' he said with a nervous grin.

'You honestly don't know anything about it?' Steve asked.

Roger didn't answer. 'Tell me,' he prompted.

'Well, I only heard it from Sarah, but I gather Hilary rang up Robin and said you wouldn't be coming in again. And that you were going away for a while.'

Roger let out a small, bitter laugh. 'Did she say where?'

'No, but . . .' Steve hesitated.

'Go on, Steve, it's all right. I can deal with it.'

'Well, when Robin went to see Hilary a few days ago she hinted you were going to some kind of nursing . . . home. Are you?'

Roger shook his head. 'I don't know. If Hilary says so, I suppose I must be.'

'But, Roger!' Steve exploded. 'This is ridiculous. You're not mad. You don't have to do anything you don't want to!'

Roger smiled at his friend. It was a sad, secret smile that hinted at the suffering only he knew was to come. The rest of the lunch hour passed in talk about the agency and the ups and downs the two of them had been through with various clients and on various campaigns.

When they said goodbye, Steve again returned to the subject of what Roger was going to do. But he got nowhere. He had looked away and started to walk back to the agency when Roger called after him.

'Steve!'

'Yes?'

'Come and visit me sometime,' Roger called, and hurried away round the corner of Whitchurch Street. It had begun to rain.

Despite the rain that grew steadily heavier, Roger spent the afternoon wandering around the West End, visiting some of the places he liked best.

So it was to be soon. Probably tonight. He knew that now. And somehow the knowledge that it would soon be over, or at least started, was comforting.

As he walked along the crowded streets, Roger could not help wondering what was going to happen. He thought of the two nurses. And Dr Willis, and shuddered.

The sky grew darker. A wind as cold as ice started to bite at his body. And Roger knew that somehow it was all a grim forewarning of whatever lay ahead.

Roger was, of course, aware that his body, or the surface of his body, was undergoing certain changes. But he didn't know how far those changes would go.

And then again, he knew that he was changing in other ways too. His senses had sharpened. His instincts were different.

Would the metamorphosis be complete? Would it even be enough? He did not think so. There had to be more. What purpose would the fantastic transformation serve by itself.

He felt sure there were further tests in store for him. Tests that would involve pain. And suffering. Roger stopped and looked at himself in a shop window. He could see the fear written on his face.

'Please God, don't let it hurt too much,' he whispered to himself. He wondered, not for the first time, whether he should throw himself under a bus. Or perhaps a tube train. That was meant to be quick, relatively painless. But Roger knew he couldn't do it.

And deep inside he knew too he would not be allowed to do it. There was to be no cheating. Payment, for whatever crime he had committed, would have to be made in full. And as if to emphasize the fact, the rain poured down and the wind bit a little deeper into his frightened body.

Judith Wright lay on the bed exhausted. Lionel had gone back to work over half an hour ago. But she could not bring herself to leave the scene of so much pleasure. It had never been so good. Lionel had never been so big and so strong.

He was like some wild animal, rutting into her. Had she imagined it, Judith asked herself, or had Lionel just for a fraction of time, actually been transformed into part-animal, part-man?

She shook her head. That was too fanciful. Too ridiculous for words. These games were beginning to affect her mind.

Judith glanced towards the window, her eye caught by a movement on the branch of the cherry tree that spread over the patio. It was a cat. It was a black cat, and it was sitting in the rain looking at her. No, not looking, Judith decided, staring. Judith stared back. Its eyes were huge. It was as if it was trying to hypnotize her. Or, perhaps, send her a message.

Judith closed her eyes and immediately found herself looking at an image of her son, Roger. But it was not the Roger she knew. Not the Roger he should be.

And then suddenly, Judith knew the meaning of what she was being shown. It was a message, a chilling one. It confirmed all her worst fears.

By the time Roger got home the rain and the wind had turned into a full-scale storm. Thunder rolled around the sky and lightning arced its way between the tall, austere Victorian buildings.

It was as he turned off the pavement towards the house that Roger heard a voice call his name. It was a woman's voice and for a moment Roger thought that Hilary must have seen him and called out to him. But there was no-one in sight and the curtains of the house were drawn, closed.

Roger stood listening for a moment, but the voice did not call again and he put it down to a trick of the wind.

Inside the house he was greeted by the delicious smell of roast chicken. And Hilary was dressed to kill.

'You're soaking wet, darling,' Hilary said. 'Go and have a bath and get into some dry clothes. I'll make us a drink.'

Roger went upstairs and turned on the taps in the bathroom. Outside the wind howled and just for a minute he thought he heard his name whispered low. But then the feeling was gone and Roger dismissed it as nerves.

The bath was hot and comforting. Roger lay back and closed his eyes and tried to relax. He knew the fine, black, silky hair had started to grow again, but he didn't want to look.

Slowly the noise of the storm seemed to die away. He felt himself go drowsy. And then, as if someone had clicked a slide into place in his head he found himself thinking about the cellar. And the grave he had dug for Ra.

The thought was followed immediately by an almost overpowering urge to go down to the cellar and see if Ra's body was in the grave. Or not.

Roger got out of the bath and started to dry himself. He heard his name being called and stiffened. What was going on? He opened the bathroom door and heard Hilary calling from downstairs.

'Your drink's ready!'

'I'll be down in a minute,' he called back and shut the bathroom door again.

He dried himself quickly and noticed that in some places the black, silky hair had grown quite considerably since the morning.

He reached the bottom of the stairs and again felt a strong urge to go down to the cellar and look for Ra's body. Somewhere in the recesses of his mind a small voice seemed to be calling him, daring him to come and see the black cat again.

Roger moved towards the cellar door but was stopped by the appearance of Hilary in the lounge door. She had a vodka and tonic in her hand.

'Here you are, darling,' she said handing it to him.

'Dinner will be ready in about ten minutes.'

Roger took the glass. 'It smells good.'

'It's chicken,' Hilary said, 'your favourite.'

They sat down on the settee and drank their drinks.

Outside the storm seemed to grow in intensity.

The wind howled viciously around the top of the house and down the narrow side passage. And at times it seemed as if the thunder would smash its way through the roof.

Yet despite the noise of the storm and the almost overpowering nearness of Hilary, the voice at the back of Roger's head kept calling his name. And the urge to go down to the cellar grew ever stronger.

The chicken was delicious. Roger couldn't remember chicken smelling or tasting so good. They were half-way through the meal when the phone rang. Hilary got up to answer it.

'I'll go, it's probably Aunt Joan. You carry on,' she said. 'Don't wait for me.'

Roger nodded. He didn't have any intention of waiting. The chicken was too good for that. He bit into a juicy bit of leg, and for no reason at all, suddenly remembered that Ra had liked chicken. On more than one occasion the cat had raided the rubbish bin after they had had chicken for dinner or Sunday lunch. And on one occasion Ra had actually stolen the food off Hilary's plate while she was out of the room.

Roger finished his meal. Hilary was still on the phone. He could hear the muted sound of her voice through the partially closed door. It sounded as if she was going to be on the phone for quite a while.

Roger looked across at her plate. There was a lot of chicken left. He half wondered if he ought to put it back in the oven, or under the grill to keep warm.

It did look good. He wondered if there was any more outside. And then he remembered that there wasn't. He'd seen Hilary put the carving dish into the washing up bowl to soak.

Roger had a sip of wine. And screwed up his nose. Strange, he wasn't really enjoying the claret this evening. He didn't really want anymore.

It was the chicken he wanted.

And then it happened. One minute he was sitting back, comfortably in his chair, the next he was bent over Hilary's plate.

Mmm! The chicken was good. Roger buried his face in the plate, pushing the vegetables out of the way, so that he could more easily get at the tender white meat.

When he had finished Hilary's chicken, Roger returned to his own chair. The chicken had been good, but now he felt ashamed and didn't know what to do when Hilary came off the phone.

The voice in his head was getting louder. Stronger. It was calling him down to the cellar. Roger wanted to go, knew that sooner or later he would have to go. But he knew there was danger, too.

He heard Hilary put down the phone in the hall and start to walk back towards the dining room. Roger picked up his knife and fork and put an imaginary piece of food in his mouth. He knew it was ridiculous to try and pretend that he hadn't eaten Hilary's chicken, but he didn't know what else to do.

Hilary sat down at the table and picked up her glass. She didn't say anything. After a minute Roger asked, 'Who was on the phone?'

'Sue.'

Roger nodded. Hilary took another sip of her wine. She didn't mention the chicken. Roger wanted to leave the table and go down to the cellar. The feeling and the voice inside his head was getting stronger.

He wondered if Hilary knew. Why didn't she mention the chicken?

'Shall we have some coffee?' Hilary suggested.

'Yes,' Roger agreed, 'that would be nice.'

He helped her take the dishes out to the kitchen.

On his way he passed the cellar door. The voice grew louder. It was coming from the cellar.

Hilary plugged in the coffee percolator and they started to wash up. She started to tell Roger about her conversation with Sue, but all Roger could hear was the voice calling him down to the cellar.

He put down the plate he was drying. And the tea towel.

'Where are you going?' Hilary asked as he started to leave the kitchen.

'I'll be back in a minute,' Roger said. 'I'm just going upstairs.' Hilary didn't say anything.

Roger closed the kitchen door behind him and walked slowly towards the cellar door. The voice was calling him all the time now.

He opened the cellar door and switched on the light. It felt cold in the cellar. Damp. It was almost as if there was a light mist swirling about at the front of the uneven steps.

Roger started down the steps. The voice was very strong now. It seemed to be all around him. Talking to him, bidding him to come. Roger knew it was Bast's voice. It spoke in a strange tongue but he understood what it was saying.

Roger reached the bottom of the steps. The mist seemed thicker. It was hard to see the walls of the cellar. And it was colder.

He wanted to go back upstairs into the warm, but the force that was calling him was so strong.

Roger started towards Ra's grave, but found himself forced instead into the centre of the cellar. He knew that he was not alone anymore. He couldn't see anyone else, it was more a question of feeling. There were lots of them, he knew that. It was like some huge invisible force.

It grew colder and Roger shivered as a great wind rose up, almost knocking him off his feet. And then, just as suddenly as it had begun, the wind died away and there standing before him was the most beautiful creature Roger had ever seen.

There were voices too, singing. And Roger knew that they were singing the praises of the goddess who stood before him.

She moved towards him and as she did her loose flowing robe fell open to reveal her naked body.

She moved closer. Roger felt the excitement grow in him. He wanted her more than he'd wanted anyone or anything in his life before.

She was close to him now. Very close. He could feel the beauty of her form. He could smell the scent of her body.

Slowly, she undid the jewelled clasp at her neck, and the golden robe fell to the floor. Roger reached forward, the blood pounding inside his excited body.

She came into his arms and he felt her hands start to stroke his body. Her touch was soft and teasing. He could feel the electricity flowing through him. He could feel his limbs jump with a surge of energy that seemed to shoot through his whole body.

He couldn't take his eyes from her. She was beautiful. She was perfection. Her hands came up and stroked his cheeks. She gently guided his face closer. Her lips were like soft, red cushions. Roger felt as if he could drown in them.

He wanted to kiss them. To kiss her.

The music rose to a crescendo, urging him on.

He was going to kiss her.

The beautiful face came nearer. Their lips touched. And then it was over. There was no more.

There was just the dark. And the cold.

And the sudden realization that in the instant of the kiss, the transformation had taken place.

He was a cat!

Chapter Sixteen

Roger did not know where he was. The darkness was complete. But he did know that he was no longer in the cellar.

He was outside, he was sure of that. But outside where? He peered into the darkness, but he could see nothing. He started to explore the area immediately around him.

The surface he was standing on felt funny. Strangely gritty. He moved slightly to his right and felt his foot sink slightly into the surface. Sand. That was it. He was standing on sand.

Before he had time to think about where the sand might be, Roger's eyes became aware of the tiniest fragment of light in the far, far distance.

Slowly at the beginning and then more rapidly, the thin line of light began to spread to the right and left until it stretched in every direction, as far as Roger could see. It was as if some invisible hand had drawn a white, glowing line round the edge of a dark world.

The light grew again, this time reaching upwards and outwards. It was like some incredible display of lightning. And it was all happening with such speed. It took only seconds for the dazzling white light to reach Roger. And when it came, the heat came with it. A dry, intense heat, that struck him suddenly like the fierce blast of an oven when the door was opened.

And as the light came, Roger saw that he was in the middle of some vast desert.

He felt the sand grow hot underneath him. And felt the life begin to drain from his body. He screwed up his eyes and looked around him, but the sun burning down on the golden whiteness of the desert blinded him.

Roger didn't understand, didn't know what to do. But he knew that he had to do something. The sun was burning into his back. His eyes were sore from the fierceness of the light. And already his mouth was dry and his body called out for water.

Without knowing why, Roger turned to his left and started to make his way slowly towards the distant horizon.

He walked for hours, turning first this way and then that as he thought he heard a noise or saw a speck in the distance that seemed to move.

His feet were sore, blistered from the heat. His tongue was swollen. He was exhausted. He wanted to sleep in the shade. And more than anything else, to drink down long, cool draughts of clear, cold water.

But he dared not stop. In the last few minutes he had noticed huge, black birds circling in the sky over him! And over to the east.

'Vultures!'

Roger remembered reading that they could smell death long before it finally claimed its unhappy victim.

He forced himself to walk on. It was like treading on burning coals. There were open sores on his feet and small grains of sand had worked their way into every crevice of his body.

Above the noise of the big black birds, Roger thought he could hear a high-pitched wailing sound. He turned to his right and started to slowly drag himself towards the sound.

The noise grew louder. And as Roger moved towards the ridge of a high dune, he became aware of the smell.

He walked on, not daring to stop. There was no alternative. Whatever lay on the other side of the ridge was preferable to the harsh heat of the desert. And the vultures!

Maybe there were houses there. And people. Maybe there was food and drink. And Roger wanted food and drink and rest more than anything in the world.

The sky above him was filled with the blackness of the vultures' ugly bodies and their huge wings that seemed to beat the air.

Roger reached the top of the big sand dune and found himself looking down on a great river. But it was a river of blood. And the land on either side of the river was stained bright red. The land was covered with the bodies of dead things and dead people. And on animal and human body alike, the vultures sat, their jaws dripping blood as they ripped at the flesh and picked the bones of the corpses.

In the distance Roger could see crowds of people standing before a huge temple or palace. They were crying out with loud voices for the Pharaoh and their gods to save them.

A sound made Roger move his head and he found himself looking straight at the obscene, blood-stained head of a vulture.

It raised its great beak and made ready to strike. And Roger knew that unless he could summon up enough strength to move, then he was about to be torn to pieces, while he was still alive.

The huge beak came seething down at him like some huge bloodied sword flashing in the sunlight.

Roger made a desperate effort to run but his shaking legs did not have the strength to respond. His whole body seemed alive with a burning pain.

The huge beak started its final descent. Already the jaws were open. Roger summoned up every drop of energy he possessed and with one enormous effort managed to twist over on to his back and roll over the top of the ridge.

He felt himself falling. Falling towards the cries of the Egyptians. And the sickening smell of death.

When he opened his eyes, Roger found himself lying in a pool of crimson blood. At first he thought that the vulture had caught him with his beak. But then he remembered the scene he had looked down on from the top of the sand dunes.

Roger looked around him. It was as if some terrible battle had been fought, with many killed and much blood lost. But on looking more closely at the awful scene that confronted him, he realized that the explanation was not as simple as he had first supposed.

For a start, there were not enough bodies to explain the vast quantities of blood. And secondly, as far as he could see from what the vultures had left, the bodies were free of any of the normal scars of war.

He started to move slowly forward, picking his way between the half-eaten corpse of a child and that of a dog. Five minutes later, Roger had joined the clamouring throng of people in front of what he now saw to be a vast Royal Palace.

The crowd were crying out to the Pharaoh and to the gods of ancient Egypt to lift the curse that had been laid upon them.

The Pharaoh, and all of his magicians, called out to the crowd that they were doing their best to lift the terrible curse, but that their magic was not strong enough.

Roger left the crowd and started to explore the village in search of food. But there was nothing. Nowhere was there a single drop of water, or wine, or milk that had not been turned to blood.

From what he had heard while he was standing in the crowd, Roger knew that the curse had lain over the land for seven days. And that many had died through lack of water and lack of food. The crops in the fields and the beasts of the land had died too, due to the great lack of water.

Two young men came into the hut where Roger was

resting. They stopped when they saw him and looked at him strangely. They whispered together and then slowly came towards him making reassuring noises, but Roger felt that they meant to harm him and was already looking for a way to escape. But why did they want to harm him? He didn't understand. One of the young men made a joke to the other, and then Roger realized that they meant to eat him.

He ran. He ran as fast as his tired, weak legs would carry him. And the young men ran after him. Other villagers joined in, chasing Roger first this way and then that, until he could run no further.

He lay exhausted on the ground listening to the noise of the oncoming crowd. But the hunters never arrived. Instead a great cry went up from all around him. A shout of joy.

Roger raised his head from the dust and saw that the ugly red stains that had covered the ground had gone. The sky was blue and free from the black clouds of vultures that had threatened to blot out the strength and blessing of the sun.

The land was clear and clean too. And Roger could see crops of barley, wheat and flax reaching up once more towards the golden light of the sun. Roger walked slowly and painfully towards the great river Nile, for it too was flowing again. He reached the reeds and the cool comfort of the muddy reed-beds and there he drank the cool water and bathed his tired and aching feet.

In the morning, Roger felt refreshed. He explored the village and scavenged some food from several of the huts.

He wanted to stay and rest further, but there was a feeling, a force, within him that seemed to drive him out into the desert again.

He made his way along the bank of the great river, stopping every so often to refresh himself with long draughts of cool water and to rest in the shade of the reeds.

Towards mid-afternoon he came to another, smaller village set back from the river edge. Roger felt a sense of relief, but no sooner had he arrived than so did a second great plague.

Boils: great swollen pustules that seemed to grow on the skin like some obscene, ripe fruit. Boils filled with a creamy, poisonous pus that burst, leaving hideous, suppurating places that spread like some ghastly white mucus over every part of the body.

And on every open place and weeping sore fed a hundred insects. Roger hid himself away not wanting to look at the hideous sight of the people as they cried for themselves and their families and their beasts. For no-one and nothing escaped the aching, throbbing, bloated growths. Not even the Pharaoh himself.

Roger made his way to where the crowd was gathered in front of the temple. The cries of the people were loud and piteous. On the steps of the temple, Roger could see the priests in their white and gold robes.

He moved through the crowd until he was at the very steps of the temple. The priests and magicians were calling out to the gods to lift the plague of boils from the land. Offerings were being prepared, wine in exquisite hand-beaten chalices was set out on a table made of pure gold. And towards the back of the platform on a magnificent, burnished throne sat the Pharaoh attended by his servants and his advisers.

But despite the incantations of the priests and the magicians, the wise men and the wizards, the obscene pustules continued to cover every living thing.

The stench was terrible. The air reeked of poison. Roger turned and ran out into the cleanness of the desert.

By night he froze and by day the terrible heat of the sun almost roasted him alive. He had lost the great river now and for two days and nights could find neither food nor drink to sustain him.

His body was weak, and the pain he felt was excruciating.

It was then Roger saw the great pyramid with its golden peak reaching up into the sun. And as he saw it, he once more heard the voice calling him to come.

The inside of the pyramid was deliciously cool after the heat of the desert. Roger found himself walking along a narrow passageway. It seemed to slope gently upwards. And from somewhere ahead of him, Roger could feel the gentlest of breezes softly kissing his fur. It seemed to carry on it a rich, almost spicy smell that made his nose twitch.

Roger moved forward cautiously up the slope and soon found himself forced to turn sharply to his left. His eyes were getting used to the dark now. And there was anyway a faint glow from what appeared to be the end of the long passage. The light was soft and uneven. And seemed to move with the breeze. The smell of spice was stronger, too.

Roger stopped and peered more closely at the walls on either side of him. He could see now that they were covered with carved figures showing scenes from what looked like early Egyptian life. They were like the wall paintings and carvings he'd seen in the British Museum.

The walls of the passage were indeed high, disappearing into darkness many feet above him. At the end of the passage, Roger was forced to turn to his left again.

There was more light now, and he could see that it came from oil lamps fixed in stone alcoves carved out of the wall. There were paintings too, of kings and queens and armies. And of gods. Roger noticed that all the gods were shown in the same form, the figures being half-human, half-animal.

The paintings and the carvings were annotated with hieroglyphics. And strangely the look of them reminded

Roger of the foreign tongue he had heard Hilary use. He felt frightened and wanted to turn back, but the voice was still urging him to come. And Roger knew he could not refuse it.

Halfway down the passageway Roger came to a huge stone doorway. A light flickered at either side of the door and Roger could see that the surface of the door carried a large painting of Bast. On her head she was wearing the double crown of Upper and Lower Egypt.

Roger sat looking at the great painting. It was beautiful. Bast was beautiful. More beautiful than any creature he had ever seen. As he gazed at the picture, Roger realized that he could hear music. Strange music with unusual rhythms and thin discordant melodies that both excited him and disturbed him at one and the same time.

Roger put out a paw and pushed tentatively at the giant door in front of him. There was a low, rumbling noise and almost immediately the huge stone slab slid back to reveal a small chamber lit by the dancing flames of oil lamps.

The room had a floor made out of the deepest blue tiles. The flickering light of the oil lamps seemed to create movement on the shiny surface of the tiles so that it reminded Roger of some great river, perhaps even the Nile itself. Inside the room the music was louder and the smell of exquisite and exotic perfumes stronger.

The walls that rose to a domed ceiling were covered with paintings of the gods. Strange gods, made stranger and more frightening by their half forms. Roger didn't understand how, but he seemed to know their names. There was Anubis with his jackal's head. Apis the bull, Khnum the ram, Sebek the crocodile, Mehit the lynx, Khepi the scarab and many, many more. But above them all, attended by a thousand slaves, rose the mighty and beautiful figure of Bast.

Bast the beautiful god. Bast who had called him to this strange place to receive punishment at her own hands.

And under the eyes of those same strange gods whose weird, almost deformed shapes decorated the walls.

Roger had been so busy examining the wall paintings that it was a while before he realized that the vast doors to the chamber had closed behind him. In fact, so perfect was the design of the chamber that he could no longer see where the door had been. Roger examined the outer walls of the chamber, anxiously scratching and sniffing at the stone. But there was no sign of a break between wall and floor. Or, for that matter, between any section of the wall.

The music had stopped. There was complete and utter silence. A stillness and a quiet that was even more chilling than the eerie musical discords that had drawn him into the chamber a few minutes before. Roger settled himself in one corner of the room. He realized with horror how quickly he had accepted his new form.

His transformation had been total, with just one exception. He was, he realized, still thinking like a human being. His brain had remained as it was. His memory was intact, and when he thought about the past, he was able to think of himself in human, rather than animal, form. And then again, his reaction to everything that had happened, that was happening to him, was a human reaction.

And then another thought struck him. What if all cats had what he called a human brain. What if the scientists had been wrong all these years? What if all animals, everywhere, could understand what was being said to them and about them?

Roger thought of Ra. He was sure Ra had understood everything, even what he, Roger, had been thinking. If he could, why not others? Or was Ra special, unique?

Roger was still trying to take in the enormity of this new thought when there was the faintest whisper of noise from the other side of the room. A small door had opened in the far wall and the almost naked body of a female creature entered the room.

Roger marvelled at her beauty. Her body was lithe and slender, her belly had a graceful swell to it and there was the perfect roundness of her breasts. But it was her face that fascinated Roger most, that held him spellbound. It was the face of a cat. A Siamese cat, but then again, it was the face of a woman, too.

When the creature spoke, her voice was low and musical. But soft though her voice was, the words she spoke brought little comfort to Roger.

'You have been brought here to the Great Pyramid to answer before Bast, the great goddess who rules our world. It is she and only she who can decide the fate of one who has dared to take life from her son and consort, Prince Ra. But first you must prepare yourself for the ordeal that is to come.'

A minute later food and drink appeared in plenty. And after Roger had fed himself, a deep, dreamless sleep that seemed to last a thousand years settled over him.

Chapter Seventeen

Carol had been amazed at what Hilary had told her. Amazed and delighted. It explained so many things. Even down to her growing feelings about Roger. She had often heard of sisters falling for the same man.

Sisters! Well almost. That's what Hilary had said. They'd had the same father, but not the same mother.

At first, just for a moment, Carol had wondered, a little jealously, why Derek hadn't married her mother instead of Hilary's. But then the thought of being Hilary's sister had driven everything else from her mind. Hilary's sister. Half-sister. And that's what Hilary said she'd be, her other half. Together they would be one. Together they would manage everything.

Hilary would have Ra and the child to look after. And, of course, she, Carol was going to help as well. But she had other duties too. Duties that concerned Roger. Hilary had explained that. That's why they had been brought together. Together they would be wife and mother, nurse and lover to the three men in the household.

Carol lay on the bed and thought about Roger. She wished he'd come back soon from wherever he was. Then, she could do with him what she could only dream about and do to herself now.

Hilary moved away from Carol's door and walked silently back to her own room. She was smiling. A smile that said it was all going to work. But then it was silly to be surprised at that. She had known since the night of the big storm it was going to be all right. For her. And for Ra.

And now there was Carol. It would be nice having a new relation, Hilary thought. Together they would be able to do anything. Everything.

She understood. She was to keep herself for Ra and the child. And later the child when he became a man. Carol would take on her love for Roger and fulfil his needs while he helped with the child's education. It was all going to be perfect, Hilary thought and wished Ra, and Roger, would hurry back.

Judith Wright didn't know what to do with herself. It was only 11 o'clock and already all she could think of was Lionel coming home for lunch, and the game they had arranged to play.

But that was two hours away and she could feel the excitement running through her body like great rivers of fire. And she didn't know what to do about it.

Judith didn't know what was happening to her. It was getting worse. She was never satisfied these days. She wondered if she was turning into a nymphomaniac. She'd read about women like that.

She tried thinking about something else, but it didn't help. The only thing that was going to help her this morning was a man. And not in two hours time.

From the front window Judith could see the milkman working his way down the street. He would be at her door in about ten minutes time.

Judith went upstairs and took off the old sweater and skirt she was wearing. From the chest of drawers she took out a black suspender belt and some silk stockings and a thin pair of pants. She took a black skirt with a split up the side from the wardrobe and a see-through blouse from the end of the bed.

Judith fluffed up her hair and put fresh lipstick on her lips. She looked at herself in the mirror. It was true what Lionel said, she was looking younger. She had lost weight, of course, but her skin seemed tauter, firmer. She didn't look much over 35.

The doorbell rang. Judith went downstairs to answer it,

not quite knowing what she was going to do. Or how she was going to do it. She hadn't thought about the milkman in that way before. She couldn't even remember how old he was or what he looked like.

She wasn't sure if it really mattered. All she wanted was a man. And she wanted, had to have, him now.

Judith opened the door and got a pleasant surprise. Jack, as she found out his name was later, was in his late thirties and not bad looking at all.

She watched his eyes notice her breasts and then flick down over the rest of her body, before returning to her face.

'One pound sixty-eight,' he said.

'My purse is in the kitchen,' Judith said. 'Actually I was just about to have a cup of coffee, would you like one?'

His eyes went down to her breasts again. She felt her nipples harden and push against the thin material. She felt more too, but Jack couldn't see that yet.

'Don't mind if I do,' he said and followed her through into the kitchen.

They drank their coffee without saying very much. Judith could feel the excitement growing between them. Jack's hands were shaking, ever so slightly. He put his cup down, rattling it on the saucer as he did so.

'Where?' he asked. His voice was thick and husky.

'Here,' Judith said. 'On the table. But hurry.'

He started to undo her blouse.

'Hurry!' Judith urged.

'My hands are shaking, I can't undo the buttons,' he said.

'Tear it,' Judith commanded. 'Tear everything.'

Jack looked at her.

'Go on,' Judith begged fiercely. 'Tear it off me!'

Jack had been gone an hour. In that time Judith had cleared up the cups, parcelled up her ripped clothes and got herself ready for Lionel. Already she was excited at the thought of what they'd agreed to do.

While she waited, Judith sipped a sherry and thought about Jack Allsop. It hadn't been bad. With a bit of practice they would be good together. He would be back, she knew that. He'd never had anyone like her before. She'd surprised herself, she'd been like a wild cat.

It was as if there was some force inside her that wouldn't be satisfied. Strange she should think of herself as a wild cat, Judith thought. Roger had talked about cats. And there had been that black cat in the garden, for the last day or two.

Judith poured herself another sherry and looked at her watch. It was 12.15. She did wish Lionel would hurry up. She'd show him a thing or two when he got home.

They came for him almost as soon as he woke. There were four of them, strange creatures, like the one who had come before. But this time they wore the features of four different animals. A lioness, a scorpion, a hawk and a cobra. They said not one word. But Roger knew he was to go with them. And he knew that at long last he was to meet Bast herself.

The creatures turned to face the hidden door and waited for Roger to stand between them. The smell of spices was strong. And the sound of music echoed quietly down the long, dark passageway. It was music from another world, played on instruments that were strange to Roger's ears. There was a rhythmic beating, a droning, a rattling, a piping sound that seemed to come from far off and carry with it strange spirits and eager cries from the twilight world of the dead.

The little group walked, shuffled and slithered down the dimly lit passages towards the very heart of the great pyramid.

Roger noticed that the walls were more richly decorated

and that there were a number of smaller chambers or ante-rooms that led off the main passage.

The procession came to a halt in front of a seemingly blank wall. The cobra lent forward and seemed to kiss with her tongue a small, jewelled place on the wall. Immediately two giant doors swung open to reveal a high ceilinged chamber of vast proportions.

It was built like some huge amphitheatre with several tiers of stone benches that led down to a small, brilliantly lit stage. On the stage, on a throne of burnished gold that seemed to cast a pure, pale yellow light over everything, sat Bast.

As the doors closed behind him, a great, swelling sound rose up as if to greet Roger. And for the first time he became aware of thousands of half-creatures whose strange half-human, half-animal forms lined the great chamber.

The chanting rose to a crescendo and then dropped away as suddenly as it had started. On the stage the cat-goddess was joined by other figures who stood in a semicircle behind her.

Roger wondered who they were and without needing to ask the question seemed to receive an answer. There was Sebeck, with his crocodile's head, Lord of Death, Sokar, the falcon, the Lord of Transformations, next to him was Hathor, the Goddess of the Soul, and Mayet, the Lord of Truth. Then came Anubis, the Lord of Spiritual Becoming, and finally the great Thoth, the ibis-headed God of Wisdom and scribe of all the gods.

From high up in the chamber trumpets sounded and the escort, with Roger in its midst moved forward, down the great steps towards the altar.

At the foot of the steps, the escort halted. Complete silence fell over the chamber. Roger waited and then at a signal from Bast, felt himself pushed forward by the commander of the escort. Roger fell forward on his knees and found himself looking up at the Great Goddess.

She was beautiful. The most beautiful thing Roger had ever seen. Her human form was cloaked in the sheerest silk, and through the gossamer thinness of the material he could see clearly the breath-taking beauty of her body.

Her face was more human than many of the other gods and goddesses in the great amphitheatre, but it was still a cat's face. Her skin had the pale delicacy of moonlight, her hair was as black as jet or ebony and her eyes were huge translucent pools of emerald green.

There was absolute quiet as Bast rose and started to speak. Roger thrilled at the sound of her voice. It was soft and low, like the sweetest music and seemed to flow into every corner of the chamber. Its soft sensuality seemed to enfold him and the husky tones sent tremors of excitement through his thin body.

'Many years ago, before recorded history, before men and his newly created gods were born, we were created. Long before man started to learn the secrets of the universe, and to abuse them, we animals were already taking part in history, recording the secrets of many different worlds.

'We have been present at every turn of history; have observed every momentous event and age unfold. You will find us in the writings of wise men through the years and in the pictures of artists as they have witnessed and recorded the earth's history.

'We are an impartial and perfect store of knowledge, knowledge that is held, safe, here in this great pyramid.

'It is knowledge that one day many worlds, as yet unborn or even undreamed of, will need.

'It is knowledge pure and undefiled by human greed and desire. It is knowledge guarded by me, Bast, the eternal God of Gods, High Priestess of our order.'

Bast's voice rose and Roger could feel the excitement in the chamber begin to rise with it.

'It is I, Bast, who with her consort and son, Ra, is born again and again through union with Ra in all his forms, in all his worlds. You have dared to interrupt this holy and inevitable process and must now accept the judgement of this order and its high court.

'But before you hear your sentence you will witness the power and the glory of Bast. The immortality of Ra and the union of the Gods.'

As Bast finished speaking, a golden bier carried shoulder high by six pallbearers led by Khnevn the high priestess, was set down before her on the altar.

Roger recognized the still, seemingly dead form on the bier as Ra. But now the body of the dead cat had taken on human shape like that of the beautiful High Priestess.

It was the face with its cruel, black handsomeness that Roger knew from his previous life.

The pallbearers stepped back and turned to face the assembled company. There was a murmur of excitement as Bast rose and with a single movement shrugged off the gossamer robe that covered her exquisite nakedness.

Roger felt the excitement run through him at the sight of her beauty. He couldn't take his eyes from her. And even without looking he knew that every creature, male and female alike, in the chamber felt the same way.

Music flooded the chamber again. But this time it was music of a different character. Its haunting themes spoke of love and a gradual quickening of the ancient rhythms made the blood race in the bodies of the assembled company.

Bast approached the still form of her dead consort. She moved slowly, sensuously, all the time obeying the rhythms of the music. For a long minute she gazed at the body of her dead lover and then, crouching low over him, started to wash his whole body.

The dead cat stirred with every teasing stroke of Bast's tongue until, finally, in one convulsive movement life seemed to return to the creature.

And as life returned, so too did the feeling and passion. Roger tried to cry out, but no sound would issue from his mouth. Instead, a shriek of horror ran round his head as he realized that Bast and Hilary were one.

He tried to look away as the beautiful creature swung herself on top of Ra and then slowly lowered herself on to his excited body.

The music quickened. And Bast responded to the urgency of its new rhythm, forcing the cat's huge phallus to slide in and out of her with ever increasing frequency.

Roger tried to look away, but some unseen force seemed to keep his eyes sharply focused on the pagan love-rites that were being enacted on the altar of gold.

As the couple reached the frenzied climax of their love act, Roger became aware of something else happening behind him.

He looked round and saw that the half-creatures who filled the chamber were now engaged in their own acts of love. It was like some huge, obscene sexual chorus as animal and human joined together in an orgy of bestial couplings.

In the shimmering, dancing, gold light of the small stage Bast's body towered briefly above Ra's before impaling itself for the last time on his hardness.

Her final cry of pleasure rose above the ecstatic cries of the audience and echoed round the domed ceiling of the chamber. It was a sound that Roger would not forget for as long as he lived. And then, as if to torture him further, Bast was standing before him, her face still flushed with passion, her body glowing with the juices of love.

Roger closed his eyes, he could not bear to look at the beautiful creature he would never again possess.

But closing his eyes was not enough. Bast came closer

still until he could feel the nakedness of her body against him. He felt her hair touch his face and heard her voice fall softly upon his ear.

'In the morning you will fight my consort, Ra, in his dark form of Shibeth the Giant Rat. You must fight well, for if you survive, the scars you carry from the fight will stay with you for the rest of your life. Now they will take you to your chamber. Eat well and rest. Prepare yourself well for what is to come.'

Roger was glad to be back on his own. The scenes of depravity he had witnessed on his way back through the main chamber had shocked and disgusted him. All he wanted was to be back in his own house, with Hilary. The way they had been before the accident. They had been looking forward to having the baby so much. Everything had been so normal. There had been nothing to prepare either of them for what was to come. Roger wondered what Hilary was doing now. Did she know where he was? What was happening to him? What was going to happen to him?

Roger thought that the answer had to be yes. Of course Hilary must know. Hilary was Bast. Bast was Hilary.

The door in the far wall slid open and handmaidens bearing trays of food and drink entered the room. Bowls fashioned from the purest gold were laid out on the dark blue, tiled floor. It was a meal fit for any god.

When the handmaidens had departed, Roger went over to the feast and started to examine the food. The smell of the strange, exotic spices filled the air and he soon found himself eating greedily from the various bowls.

Later a curious sense of well-being came over him and he fell into a deep sleep. It was a sleep filled with the sweetest of dreams, as if the gods were trying to compensate him for the ordeal that lay ahead.

He dreamed of life in a strange, beautiful land, full of green valleys and high hills. There were trees bearing exotic fruits and cold, clear water that ran from the sweetest of springs. And with him, all the while, was Hilary. Or, was it Bast? Roger didn't know. The two were one now.

Once he woke, only for a minute, but he could have sworn that he saw Bast, caught in the flickering light, stealing away from his side.

The fight took place in the same huge chamber that had housed the previous night's spectacle. A small pit lined with smooth stone lay revealed in the centre of the small stage.

Behind the pit, facing out towards the auditorium was ranged a semicircle of seats. And in the centre seat sat Bast. The rest of the auditorium was filled to capacity with the same half-creatures from the previous day. There was a tremor of excitement in the air, a hush of expectancy as Roger was led down the long flight of steps to the small, brightly lit stage. And the pit.

As the procession came to a halt in front of the stage, a thin wailing sound rose up from the packed chamber. Roger thought it sounded like the cry of dead souls.

The guards pushed Roger forward towards the edge of the pit. It was then that the smell hit him. A great, filthy stench that drove him back into the arms of his captors. But there was to be no reprieve. Once again the guards pushed him forward to the edge of the pit, this time at spear point.

Roger felt the vomit surge up in his mouth and the hair on his back begin to rise. He moved forward, cautiously, encouraged by the sharpness of the weapons at his back.

The lights in the auditorium went out one by one, until there was just a single light left burning above the pit.

Brighter and brighter it burned, until it was like some brilliant spotlight shining down into the evil-smelling blackness.

The rat was huge. It was in the far corner of the pit. It

sat in its own filth, dribbling and slobbering as its tiny eyes gazed up at its intended victim. Roger flattened himself on the ground and let out a low, rumbling growl. The rat tensed itself and drew back its thick blubbery lips to reveal razor-sharp incisors.

Roger sensed rather than saw a signal made by Bast, and found himself propelled into the foul-smelling pit. The rat stayed in his corner watching Roger's every move with beady, bright eyes that peered out of folds of puffy, pink flesh.

Roger made for the safety of the walls farthest from Shibeth. The vileness of the smell all around him made him vomit. His legs were shaking, but before he had time to recover, the rat, urged on by the shouts of the crowd, started towards him.

Roger arched his back and hissed and spat at the filthy creature. But still it came on.

'Shibeth! Shibeth!' the crowd chanted.

Roger flicked out a paw and caught the rat down the side of his face. Blood spurted out of the jagged tear made by Roger's claw.

The rat paused for a moment and licked at its cheek in an effort to stop the blood before returning to the attack. Roger flicked out a paw again, but this time Shibeth was ready for him. The rat's jaws opened and closed again with incredible speed, trapping Roger's front leg as they did so.

Roger screamed with pain as the rat's teeth cut through the flesh to the bone. The rat's jaws opened as it prepared to strike again and somehow Roger managed to pull back his torn and bleeding leg.

But Shibeth had tasted blood and as Roger turned and ran the giant rat struck again, this time catching Roger high up on the thigh.

The crowd cheered as the cat cried out in pain. And, for a moment, as if to acknowledge the acclaim, Shibeth paused and blinked up at the bright overhead light.

Roger turned to face the evil-smelling vermin. He was weak and the pain in his front and back legs was making him dizzy. He was losing blood and he knew that unless he killed the rat quickly, he was finished.

The rat smelt the fear that ran through Roger's body and tasted Roger's blood on its obscenely large claws. It knew it would win. It was only a matter of time.

The two animals stared at each other across the blood-stained floor of the pit. And then, as if in response to some secret signal they both launched a furious attack.

Even as he felt his own claws rip into Shibeth's flesh, Roger felt the rat's claws slide across his face, pulling flesh away from bone and separating his eye from its socket. Roger bit into the bloated flesh of the rat's throat and tasted blood. He struck again, clawing furiously with sound and wounded leg alike in a desperate final effort to kill the giant rat.

But Shibeth was strong. His jaws fastened on Roger's neck and with one shake of his head he flung the cat to the far corner of the pit.

Roger lay on his side, his half-severed leg folded uselessly under him.

The crowd rose shouting to Shibeth to kill.

Roger tried to move, but his legs would not support him. All he could do was to wait for the rat to come and kill him.

The smell of the creature's putrid breath grew stronger. Roger could hear the rat making obscene, excited noises as it shuffled towards him. He tried to stop the blood pumping down his face, but it was flowing too fast. Perhaps it didn't matter, he thought to himself.

It would all be over very soon now.

And then the blood cleared from Roger's good eye and he saw Shibeth leaning over him, saliva running down the side of his already blood-stained mouth.

The rat's jaws opened. The obscene, slobbering mouth

moved towards its prey. All Roger could think about was the release from pain the gods were about to grant him.

But it was not to be, for as Shibeth made his final strike, Roger heard the soft, low voice of Bast call to the creature to hold back.

And then he lost consciousness.

Chapter Eighteen

Carol had taken a lot of trouble with her appearance. After all it was a special day for her. She was excited. She was going to see Roger and soon her real job would begin.

Hilary hadn't told her what had happened, just that Roger was in hospital. Carol had tried to find out more, but Hilary would not be drawn.

'Well, what exactly is wrong with him?' she asked, changing the direction of her questioning.

'I don't know the full extent of his injuries,' Hilary said quietly. And she was telling the truth. Of course, she had known that Roger, when he returned, would need looking after. But she did not know how he had been injured or how serious those injuries were.

All Hilary knew for sure was that during the night, something, or things, had happened that had finally changed all their lives.

She had woken twice during the night. The first time to find herself having an orgasm that was so fierce it had made her clutch at the brass bedhead for support. On the second occasion she thought she had heard a scream and had got up to see if Carol was having a nightmare. But she was not.

When Hilary had gone back to her room, Ra was there. Asleep on the end of the bed, where, a minute before, Hilary had been sleeping. He had stayed close to her for the rest of the night.

The visit from the police had come at 9.30 in the morning. A Sergeant Dicks, he was a nice man. He'd made her sit down and asked Carol to make a cup of tea.

He'd asked her when she'd last seen Roger. And she told him it had been the previous night. At dinner.

'What about after dinner?' Sergeant Dicks asked. 'What happened then?'

'He went to his study to do some work.'

'And what happened after that?'

'He said he might go for a walk,' Hilary replied. 'He had a headache.'

'And what did you do, Mrs Wright?'

'I went to bed. I was tired. Roger said he'd sleep in the spare room if he came up late, so as not to wake me.'

'And did he?' Sergeant Dicks asked.

'I suppose he must have.'

'You don't know for sure?'

'No.'

'What about this morning, did you see him then?'

Hilary shook her head.

'What about you, Mrs Coren?'

Carol shook her head. 'No, I haven't seen him since I moved here. What's happened to him? Why are you asking us all these questions?'

'What has happened, Sergeant?' Hilary asked.

'I'm afraid your husband's in a bad way, Mrs Wright. He was found early this morning on some waste ground near St Michael's Hospital. In a fine old state he was. We don't know what happened to him but he looks as if he's been in a fight with a wild animal. It's going to be a bit of a shock for you, Mrs Wright.'

Hilary said she would go to the hospital straight away, but the policeman had persuaded her not to. They were operating and it would be several hours before they would know for sure the full extent of Roger's injuries. If she would ring the hospital later they would tell her when she could see her husband.

Husband? It sounded strange. Hilary supposed that was because she no longer regarded Roger as her husband. She was married to Ra now. Although she still needed Roger for some things.

It was Carol who had rung the hospital. Several times. At first there had been no news. But finally, at 5 o'clock, the sister had said they could come over at 7.

They had been met by Dr Lee and taken to a small room on the first floor. The doctor looked grim.

'I'm afraid you're in for a bit of a shock, Mrs Wright. Your husband's not a pretty sight. Lord knows what happened to him. I haven't seen injuries like this in all the time I've been practising medicine.'

'What exactly is the matter with him, Doctor?'

It was Carol who asked the question.

'Well, we've had to take his left leg off above the knee. We've amputated the right arm at the elbow. He's lost his left eye and I'm afraid that even with plastic surgery the rest of his face and neck will never be a very pleasant sight. There are other scars on the abdomen, stomach and chest. But, of course, they can be covered.'

Hilary didn't say anything. She just sat quietly and nodded her acceptance.

It was Carol who cried.

'I expect you'd like to see him?' Dr Lee asked.

'Yes,' Hilary replied.

'He's pretty heavily sedated so I don't know what you'll get out of him. The police are anxious to speak to him when he recovers, but that will be several days yet. I suggest you only stay for a few minutes on this first visit.'

Roger was in a small room on the second floor. His condition was too serious for him to be put in a general ward. He had heard Dr Lee talking to his colleagues earlier. He had heard too what they had done to him in the operating theatre.

A leg, an arm and an eye. And a mess for a face. He wondered how Hilary would like that. He understood them punishing him, condemning him to some sort of half life, but what effect was it going to have on Hilary? Surely they could have found some equally savage punishment for him that would have left her free.

But then he was forgetting, Hilary was Bast, or was she?

He heard a clock strike and then the sound of the door opening. He knew it was Hilary before he heard her voice. There was something in the air.

There was a man's voice, probably the doctor's, and a woman's voice and then Hilary's. Soft and low, it came spinning round the room towards him.

He tried to shut it out but it wouldn't go away. And then Hilary was there beside him. Very close. He could feel her hair on that bit of his face that was not covered in bandages.

'Roger,' she whispered, 'I've got some news for you. Carol, you remember Carol Coren, don't you? Well, she's come to live with us and she's going to spend all her time looking after you. She says she'll do everything for you, everything. So you don't have to worry. And you'll never guess, Ra's back. And he sends his love. And Roger, there's something else . . . I'M GOING TO HAVE A BABY. So you see you must hurry up and get well and come home because we're all waiting for you. We're all going to be one big happy family.'

Roger didn't answer. And after a minute he heard the doctor whisper to Hilary that perhaps it would be a good idea if she left now.

He felt her come close again. And smelt her perfume. And something else, the musk of her body. It brought back memories of Bast. Roger tensed himself as Hilary bent low over him. She kissed his head and whispered goodbye.

When they'd all gone, Roger tried to sort things out in his mind. Despite the drugs they had pumped into him his mind was very clear. And he realized too, that some of the extra senses he'd seemed to be given in his cat life, were still with him. It was as if he was two beings. Or, half-human, half-cat.

Yes, that was it. And suddenly with overwhelming clarity Roger knew the answer to everything. It was the child, of course. And Ra. The god in both his forms needed a father. Someone who would help and guide the young child in both his lives.

And in return, Roger had his life. Just. Would he be allowed to earn some of his missing limbs back again, he wondered. He had no doubt that the family, as Hilary called it, would be provided for, somehow. He wondered if he would be involved.

What he did know was that for the time being, he was their prisoner. They had forced the bargain on him, given him no chance to refuse.

He would have to play whatever role they demanded of him. Because he was one of them now. A half-creature.

Or was he?

Roger could feel the scream start deep inside him, slowly it seemed to run round his broken body and his scarred head.

And then it burst from his thin, white bandaged mouth. It was a terrible sound that echoed round the whole hospital.

A cry, half-human, half something else.

A caterwaul.